TOEIC

練習測驗（7）

LISTENING TEST

In the Listening test, you will be asked to demonstrate how well you understand spoken English. The entire Listening test will last approximately 45 minutes. There are four parts, and directions are given for each part. You must mark your answers on the separate answer sheet. Do not write your answers in your test book.

PART 1

Directions: For each question in this part, you will hear four statements about a picture in your test book. When you hear the statements, you must select the one statement that best describes what you see in the picture. Then find the number of the question on your answer sheet and mark your answer. The statements will not be printed in your test book and will be spoken only one time.

Statement (C), "They're sitting at a table," is the best description of the picture, so you should select answer (C) and mark it on your answer sheet.

1.

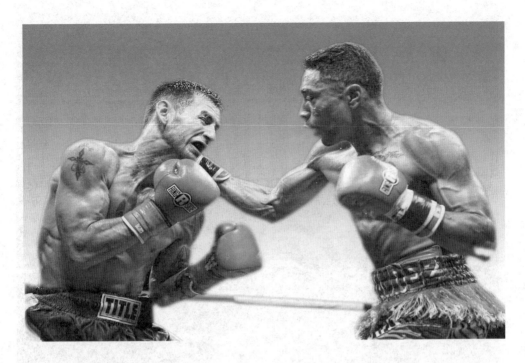

2.

GO ON TO THE NEXT PAGE.

3.

4.

5.

6.

GO ON TO THE NEXT PAGE.

PART 2

Directions: You will hear a question or statement and three responses spoken in English. They will not be printed in your test book and will be spoken only one time. Select the best response to the question or statement and mark the letter (A), (B), or (C) on your answer sheet.

7. Mark your answer on your answer sheet.

8. Mark your answer on your answer sheet.

9. Mark your answer on your answer sheet.

10. Mark your answer on your answer sheet.

11. Mark your answer on your answer sheet.

12. Mark your answer on your answer sheet.

13. Mark your answer on your answer sheet.

14. Mark your answer on your answer sheet.

15. Mark your answer on your answer sheet.

16. Mark your answer on your answer sheet.

17. Mark your answer on your answer sheet.

18. Mark your answer on your answer sheet.

19. Mark your answer on your answer sheet.

20. Mark your answer on your answer sheet.

21. Mark your answer on your answer sheet.

22. Mark your answer on your answer sheet.

23. Mark your answer on your answer sheet.

24. Mark your answer on your answer sheet.

25. Mark your answer on your answer sheet.

26. Mark your answer on your answer sheet.

27. Mark your answer on your answer sheet.

28. Mark your answer on your answer sheet.

29. Mark your answer on your answer sheet.

30. Mark your answer on your answer sheet.

31. Mark your answer on your answer sheet.

Directions: You will hear some conversations between two people. You will be asked to answer three questions about what the speakers say in each conversation. Select the best response to each question and mark the letter (A), (B), (C), or (D) on your answer sheet. The conversation will not be printed in your test book and will be spoken only one time.

32. What is the man interested in doing?
(A) Teaching a class.
(B) Contacting a landscape designer.
(C) Starting a vegetable garden.
(D) Purchasing gardening tools.

33. What does the woman suggest?
(A) Using a Web site.
(B) Visiting a different store.
(C) Purchasing a book.
(D) Attending a class.

34. What does the woman give the man?
(A) A list of courses.
(B) A textbook.
(C) Free samples.
(D) Contact information.

35. Who most likely are the speakers?
(A) Manufacturing supervisors.
(B) Automobile mechanics.
(C) Advertising executives.
(D) Mobile phone service plan salespeople.

36. What problem are the speakers discussing?
(A) Management directives have been inconsistent.
(B) A business has been losing sales.
(C) New products have received poor reviews.
(D) The sales department is understaffed.

37. What solution does the woman suggest?
(A) Soliciting customer feedback.
(B) Advertising online.
(C) Offering incentives to customers.
(D) Hiring additional staff.

38. Why was the woman late?
(A) She had to wait for transportation.
(B) She was helping a colleague.
(C) She lost her conference badge.
(D) She went to the wrong location.

39. What does the woman ask about?
(A) Some equipment rentals.
(B) A registration procedure.
(C) Some changes to a schedule.
(D) The number of attendees.

40. What does the man say?
(A) The woman may need more fliers.
(B) The woman may have missed her session.
(C) Fewer people attend morning sessions.
(D) More people will attend tomorrow.

41. Why is the man calling?
(A) A name is misspelled.
(B) A Web site is not working.
(C) A shipment is late.
(D) A product is damaged.

42. What does the man request?
(A) A tracking number.
(B) A refund.
(C) A replacement.
(D) A catalog.

43. What will the woman do next?
(A) Check an inventory.
(B) Call a warehouse.
(C) Talk to her manager.
(D) Set up an appointment.

GO ON TO THE NEXT PAGE.

44. Where is the conversation most likely taking place?
    (A) At a restaurant.
    (B) At a farmer's market.
    (C) At a flower shop.
    (D) At a tourist center.

45. According to American woman, what is true about the product?
    (A) It is locally grown.
    (B) It is new this season.
    (C) It is currently discounted.
    (D) It is only available today.

46. What is the British woman concerned about?
    (A) Supporting local producers.
    (B) Freshness of salad ingredients.
    (C) Prices of avocados.
    (D) Uses for avocados.

47. What is the woman inquiring about?
    (A) Extra baggage fees.
    (B) Flight arrival times.
    (C) Payment option.
    (D) A ticket upgrade.

48. What does the woman mean by "That's cutting it a bit close"?
    (A) She needs to be there earlier.
    (B) She wants more options.
    (C) She has already bought a ticket.
    (D) She is happy with the service she received.

49. What does the man recommend?
    (A) Using a credit card.
    (B) Speaking to a manager.
    (C) Purchasing some travel insurance.
    (D) Taking a different route.

50. What is the main topic of the conversation?
    (A) An executive's retirement.
    (B) A budget review.
    (C) A conference presentation.
    (D) A company relocation.

51. What does the man mean by "don't spill the beans"?
    (A) Arrive early at an event.
    (B) Keep some information secret.
    (C) Check an account.
    (D) Reserve a room.

52. What will the woman be doing at four o'clock on the day of the event?
    (A) Interviewing for a new job.
    (B) Meeting a client.
    (C) Completing a report.
    (D) Attending a party.

53. What problem does the woman inform the man about?
    (A) She lost her computer.
    (B) Her luggage did not arrive.
    (C) Her password is incorrect.
    (D) She missed a flight.

54. What does the man suggest?
    (A) Joining a meeting by videoconference.
    (B) Returning to a hotel.
    (C) Consulting a travel agency.
    (D) Using a car service to visit a client.

55. What does the woman plan to do next?
    (A) Report a complaint.
    (B) Go to a repair shop.
    (C) Check for some equipment.
    (D) Call an airline.

56. What is the man concerned about?
- (A) A scheduling conflict.
- (B) A missing part.
- (C) Poor sales figures.
- (D) Repairing furniture.

57. What complaint do customers have?
- (A) A product is difficult to install.
- (B) A Web site is confusing.
- (C) Deliveries are late.
- (D) Selection is limited.

58. What does the man suggest doing?
- (A) Designing a survey.
- (B) Sending an e-mail.
- (C) Canceling an order.
- (D) Offering a discount.

---

59. Why did the man call Ms. Sanchez?
- (A) To book a hotel room.
- (B) To confirm an appointment.
- (C) To reschedule a meeting.
- (D) To make a dining reservation.

60. What is located in the west annex of the hotel?
- (A) A bank.
- (B) A restaurant.
- (C) A fitness center.
- (D) A concierge.

61. According to the woman, what can the man pick up at the front desk?
- (A) A parking pass.
- (B) A discount coupon.
- (C) Travel brochure.
- (D) A registration form.

From:	Phil Bates <p_bates@alliedindustries.com>
To:	Jenna Oliver <jenna74@heatmail.com>
Re:	Interview Process
Date:	December 15

Hi Jenna,

As I mentioned in our phone conversation, here are a few details about the interview process.

- Please arrive at our offices at least 10 minutes prior to your scheduled interview.
- Attire is business casual.
- Bring two copies of your updated resume.
- Print out a list of at least three (3) character references including the following information: (A) the person's name and full contact details (email, phone); (B) your relationship; (C) a short description of how long you've known this person.

See you on Friday.

Regards,
Phil Bates

62. Why is the man calling?
- (A) To remind a customer.
- (B) To schedule an interview.
- (C) To request some sales.
- (D) To respond to a message.

63. What does the woman inquire about?
- (A) The cost of an item.
- (B) An application requirement.
- (C) An insurance policy.
- (D) The name of a company.

64. Look at the graphic. When should Jenna Oliver arrive at Allied Industries office?
- (A) 2:10.
- (B) 1:15.
- (C) 1:50.
- (D) 2:00.

GO ON TO THE NEXT PAGE.

Nutritional Information

Serving size: 250 grams

Calories 178

Amount per serving

Fat	7 grams
Protein	12 grams
Fiber	55 grams
Sodium	65 milligrams
Sugar	33 grams

TIMEZONE ELECTRONICS | discount coupon

Batteries

Cylindrical $2 off
Non- Cylindrical alkaline $3 off
All other batteries $5 off

Redeemable at any participating TIMEZONE ELECTRONICS
Expires: November 30

timezone.com

65. Why is the woman looking for a certain product?
(A) She wants to lose weight.
(B) She has an allergy to certain foods.
(C) She wants to eat healthy.
(D) She has a favorite brand.

66. Look at the graphic. Which of the ingredients does the woman express concern about?
(A) Sugar.
(B) Fat.
(C) Sodium.
(D) Fiber.

67. What does the man suggest the woman do?
(A) Try a free sample.
(B) Go to a different store.
(C) Buy a different item.
(D) Speak with her doctor.

68. What problem does the man mention?
(A) He can't find an item.
(B) He wants to return an item.
(C) A product is defective.
(D) A coupon has expired.

69. What does the woman say is currently happening?
(A) New employees are being trained.
(B) Merchandise is being relocated.
(C) Watch batteries are being discontinued.
(D) A major sale is being held.

70. Look at the graphic. What discount will the man most likely receive?
(A) Buy one get one free.
(B) 50%.
(C) $3.
(D) $5.

PART 4

Directions: You will hear some talks given by a single speaker. You will be asked to answer three questions about what the speaker says in each talk. Select the best response to each question and mark the letter (A), (B), (C), or (D) on your answer sheet. The talks will not be printed in your test book and will be spoken only one time.

71. Why does the speaker call the listener?
(A) To ask him to return some merchandise.
(B) To invite him to a writing seminar.
(C) To offer him a membership card.
(D) To notify him that a book is available.

72. What can the listener request?
(A) A private tour.
(B) Additional time.
(C) A certificate of completion.
(D) E-mail notifications.

73. What does the speaker remind the listener about?
(A) A charity event.
(B) Parking restrictions.
(C) Reduced operating hours.
(D) An application requirement.

74. Where does the speaker most likely work?
(A) At a furniture store.
(B) At a real estate company.
(C) At a construction company.
(D) At a custom bicycle shop.

75. What problem does the speaker report?
(A) An account was mistakenly closed.
(B) A factory has stopped production.
(C) A shipment is delayed.
(D) A component is unavailable.

76. What does the speaker offer to do?
(A) Refund a purchase.
(B) Meet with a customer.
(C) Send some information.
(D) Negotiate with a supplier.

77. Where most likely are the listeners?
(A) At a restaurant.
(B) At a supermarket.
(C) At a clothing boutique.
(D) At a train station.

78. What are the speaker's instructions mainly about?
(A) Some staffing assignments.
(B) Some misplaced equipment.
(C) A revised corporate policy.
(D) A computer program feature.

79. What does the speaker imply when he says, "Walter's here today"?
(A) Business is slower than usual.
(B) Staff will be observed by a supervisor.
(C) Walter made a scheduling mistake.
(D) Walter can assist with a problem.

80. What is being discussed?
(A) Internet availability.
(B) Staff retention.
(C) Luggage restrictions.
(D) Food quality.

81. What is Orion West Airlines hoping to do?
(A) Add international destinations.
(B) Upgrade a computer system.
(C) Join a partnership.
(D) Increase ticket sales.

82. What are the listeners asked to review?
(A) A budget report.
(B) A contract.
(C) A marketing video.
(D) A newspaper article.

GO ON TO THE NEXT PAGE

83. What information should the listeners look for on a Web site?
    (A) A traffic update.
    (B) A weather forecast.
    (C) Admission fees.
    (D) An event schedule.

84. Why is the event at Beacon Street Café expected to be popular?
    (A) A famous chef will be preparing meals.
    (B) The tourism board heavily advertised it.
    (C) A musician will give a concert.
    (D) The restaurant has a good reputation.

85. Why does the speaker say, "Beacon Street Café does not take reservations"?
    (A) To clarify a policy change.
    (B) To suggest arriving early.
    (C) To criticize a business.
    (D) To propose a different location.

86. What is the purpose of the message?
    (A) To submit an additional order.
    (B) To ask for directions to a factory.
    (C) To request an estimate.
    (D) To complain about a delivery.

87. Why does the speaker mention a Web site?
    (A) It is difficult to navigate.
    (B) It needs a page for feedback.
    (C) It has incorrect information.
    (D) It is currently inaccessible.

88. What does the speaker request?
    (A) A copy of an invoice.
    (B) A return telephone call.
    (C) Another machine part.
    (D) A replacement manual.

89. What kind of business do the listeners most likely work for?
    (A) An accounting firm.
    (B) A law office.
    (C) An advertising company.
    (D) A travel agency.

90. What news does the speaker share with the listeners?
    (A) A ground-breaking ceremony will be held.
    (B) A celebration is being planned.
    (C) An important client will be visiting.
    (D) The department is looking to expand.

91. What does the speaker ask the listeners to submit by the end of the day?
    (A) Color schemes for a waiting room.
    (B) Requests for vacation leave.
    (C) Time preferences for a dinner.
    (D) Items to include on a budget.

92. What is the main topic of the broadcast?
    (A) A local election.
    (B) A city government building.
    (C) Online advertising.
    (D) Public transportation.

93. What will the listeners now be able to do?
    (A) Pay a reduced fee.
    (B) Review a document.
    (C) Track some vehicles.
    (D) File a complaint electronically.

94. Why does the speaker say, "I'm going to download it today'?
    (A) To recommend a service.
    (B) To emphasize a deadline.
    (C) To take responsibility for a task.
    (D) To explain a process.

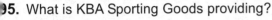

Barnum Trails Hike-A-Thon	
Barnum Edge	5 kilometers
Barnum Delta	7.5 kilometers
Barnum Trek	10 kilometers
Barnum Ultra	15 kilometers

95. What is KBA Sporting Goods providing?
(A) Prizes.
(B) Refreshments.
(C) Sports equipment.
(D) Entertainment.

96. Look at the graphic. Which route is closed?
(A) Barnum Edge.
(B) Barnum Delta.
(C) Barnum Trek.
(D) Barnum Ultra.

97. What are the participants reminded to do?
(A) Follow designated trail paths.
(B) Make a donation to an organization.
(C) Register for an upcoming event.
(D) Follow the directions of the officials.

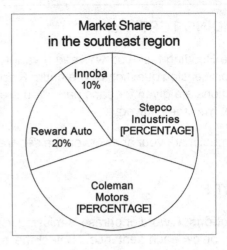

Market Share
in the southeast region

Innoba 10%

Stepco Industries [PERCENTAGE]

Reward Auto 20%

Coleman Motors [PERCENTAGE]

98. According to the speaker, what was mentioned in the company newsletter?
(A) Product sales are higher than expected.
(B) Some executives have retired.
(C) The company will open offices abroad.
(D) The company was bought by a larger firm.

99. What problem does the speaker mention?
(A) Competition has become more intense.
(B) Customers are dissatisfied.
(C) Energy costs have increased.
(D) The production capacity is limited.

100. Look at the graphic. Which company may be acquired?
(A) Reward Auto.
(B) Innoba.
(C) Coleman Motors.
(D) Stepco Industries.

This is the end of the Listening test. Turn to Part 5 in your test book.

GO ON TO THE NEXT PAGE.

READING TEST

In the Reading test, you will read a variety of texts and answer several different types of reading comprehension questions. The entire Reading test will last 75 minutes. There are three parts, and directions are given for each part. You are encouraged to answer as many questions as possible within the time allowed.

You must mark your answers on the separate answer sheet. Do not write your answers in your test book.

PART 5

Directions: A word or phrase is missing in each of the sentences below. Four answer choices are given below each sentence. Select the best answer to complete the sentence. Then mark the letter (A), (B), (C), or (D) on your answer sheet.

101. Corporate policy states that laptops, tablets, and other company ------- are not for private use.
(A) property
(B) substance
(C) rules
(D) quality

102. The taxi fare to the ferry terminal was ------- than expected because the driver knew a shortcut.
(A) now that
(B) less of
(C) little more
(D) slightly less

103. Review ------- terms of the contract carefully before signing on the final page.
(A) whole
(B) complete
(C) all
(D) each

104. ------- evaluating several delivery options, Mr. Perkins decided to send the package by local courier.
(A) After
(B) Until
(C) If
(D) Beside

105. Mr. Coburn's travel schedule is always booked solid, ------- of the season.
(A) regarding
(B) regard
(C) regardless
(D) regarded

106. Travelers should plan for longer delays than usual tomorrow because heavy rain -------.
(A) is predicted
(B) was predicting
(C) predicts
(D) prediction

107. The event organizer chose trophies for the athletes that were made of alloy metals because ------- gold is too soft.
(A) pure
(B) single
(C) rich
(D) quiet

108. Leslie O'Brien has submitted her ------- after nearly 25 years of reporting for *The Tulsa Chronicle*.
(A) resigned
(B) resignation
(C) resign
(D) resigning

109. Corvalis Allied Bank customers can easily transfer funds from one account to -------.
(A) one
(B) it
(C) another
(D) either

110. ------- a few members did not renew their subscriptions for this year, the past quarter has been very successful.
(A) Even though
(B) On the contrary
(C) Despite
(D) Moreover

111. Ms. Stevenson has promised ------- all questions about the new vacation policy in a company-wide e-mail.
(A) will answer
(B) to answer
(C) answering
(D) answer

112. Creative Aim Consulting requires its employees to respond to e-mails as ------- as possible.
(A) quicken
(B) quickest
(C) quicker
(D) quickly

113. ------- scheduled to appear at tomorrow's sales conference have been listed on the event's Web site.
(A) Rooms
(B) Presenters
(C) Notes
(D) Targets

114. Before assembling the new desk, make sure the floor beneath is completely -------.
(A) flatter
(B) flatten
(C) flat
(D) flatly

115. Passengers are required to check in forty-five minutes ------- their scheduled departure times.
(A) within
(B) before
(C) into
(D) over

116. Access to Paramount Road will be ------- to southbound traffic after the road repair project begins next month.
(A) limited
(B) limiting
(C) limit
(D) limitable

117. At Napoli Bistro, we take customer service seriously, so please remember to treat all guests with genuine -------.
(A) requirement
(B) courtesy
(C) achievement
(D) conference

118. The conference rooms on the North Campus are available only ------- afternoon functions.
(A) for
(B) in
(C) at
(D) to

119. Rhodan Bicycles can be purchased online and shipped ------- to consumers.
(A) direction
(B) directing
(C) directly
(D) directed

120. For $25, get a personalized message ------- on a piece of Carrington gold jewelry.
(A) registered
(B) progressed
(C) polished
(D) engraved

GO ON TO THE NEXT PAGE.

121. During the design contest, the judges' identities will be kept ------- and will be revealed only after a winner has been announced.
    (A) curious
    (B) missing
    (C) careful
    (D) secret

122. The intake filters of your Unger air conditioning unit must be routinely ------- to keep the appliance functioning properly.
    (A) have cleaned
    (B) clean
    (C) cleaned
    (D) of cleaning

123. Mr. Garcia will give the presentation to Vivacon's representatives ------- since he has worked with them on previous campaigns.
    (A) his
    (B) himself
    (C) he
    (D) him

124. The mayor's press conference meeting ended so ------- that few reporters were allowed to ask questions.
    (A) practically
    (B) abruptly
    (C) obviously
    (D) broadly

125. The next Technology Expo will open on a date that ------- the software developer's tenth anniversary.
    (A) inquires about
    (B) responds to
    (C) coincides with
    (D) translates to

126. If a virus makes it into one user group, it will affect not only those computers ------- the entire network.
    (A) just as
    (B) but also
    (C) provided that
    (D) even if

127. Ferguson Laboratories has announced the development of a ------- lifesaving drug to treat diabetes.
    (A) formally
    (B) originally
    (C) carefully
    (D) potentially

128. Many companies strive to be ranked among the region's best workplaces ------- attract the best job candidates.
    (A) so that
    (B) causing
    (C) towards
    (D) in order to

129. All existing recruitment efforts must be reviewed ------- the funding cuts announced yesterday by the budget committee.
    (A) as a result
    (B) because of
    (C) in front of
    (D) across from

130. Although Hurricane Stephan is not ------- to make landfall on Saturday, the Forester Company annual picnic has been postponed until August 3.
    (A) likely
    (B) likes
    (C) liking
    (D) likeness

Directions: Read the texts that follow. A word or phrase is missing in some of the sentences. Four answer choices are given below each of the sentences. Select the best answer to complete the text. Then mark the letter (A), (B), (C), or (D) on your answer sheet.

Questions 131-134 refer to the following notice.

Levis Laboratories 3-D Printer Policy

This 3-D printer is for the ------- use of Production Department employees.
       131.

Workers from other departments must use the standard printers found on

the second floor. Production Department staff members may print up to 5

objects per week without a manager's authorization. Staff must receive

managerial approval to make ------- items.
                 132.

Note that 3-D printing ------- for development and business purposes only.
          133.

No personal printing is permitted. -------.
                    134.

Thank you for your cooperation.

131. (A) peculiar
(B) unusual
(C) customary
(D) exclusive

132. (A) additional
(B) required
(C) such
(D) these

133. (A) is intended
(B) should intend
(C) intends
(D) intending

134. (A) The black-and-white printers have been upgraded to make a limited number of color copies
(B) The second-floor printers will be replaced during the month of September
(C) Objects created with the 3-D printer are for internal use by Levis Labs and external marketing associates
(D) Technical Support maintains all printers and copiers

GO ON TO THE NEXT PAGE.

From:	Gerard James <james@louisville.org.gov>
To:	Wendy Crowder <crowder@rapture.com>
Re:	Membership
Date:	October 5

Dear Ms. Crowder,

I hope you are enjoying your Louisville Museum of Natural History membership. Please note that your membership ------- on December 1.
                                                                                       135.
By renewing your membership now, you can take advantage of a special 25 percent discount.

This offer is good only ------- October 31. Simply enter the code AUGI44
                         136.
at the checkout page by this date. All of us at the Louisville Museum of Natural History appreciate your past support and hope you renew soon so that you may continue to receive all the benefits of membership without -------.
        137.

And remember, our members receive two complimentary tickets to our featured exhibition, Ancient Egyptian Artifacts. -------. As a member,
                                                                    138.
you can preview it at a special reception on November 27.

Sincerely,
Gerard James
Director of Membership
www.louisville.org.gov

135. (A) has expired
(B) will expire
(C) to be expiring
(D) must have expired

136. (A) inside
(B) against
(C) excluding
(D) until

137. (A) interrupting
(B) interruption
(C) interrupts
(D) interrupted

138. (A) Rather, we will announce the changes on November 15.
(B) We thank you for completing the membership survey.
(C) Our membership fees have increased this year.
(D) This exhibition opens to the public on December 3.

From:	Maggie Green <butterfly77@hugmail.com>
To:	Customer Support <support@shazamtech.com>
Re:	Order ST-0081294
Date:	April 12

To Whom It May Concern,

I recently purchased a pair of shoes from the Wox Tech Web site. When I first received the shoes a month and a half ago, I tried them on. -------, when I went to wear them for the first time yesterday, I
139.
noticed slight imperfections in the stitching of both toecaps.

I know that any ------- items must be returned or exchanged within
140.
three days and that my purchase is no longer within the required time frame. -------.
141.

If the shoes ------- out, I would be happy to choose another pair of
142.
shoes at the same price.

Please let me know what my options are.

Sincerely,
Maggie Green

---

139. (A) Still
(B) However
(C) Therefore
(D) Additionally

140. (A) accepted
(B) ill-fitting
(C) mistaken
(D) defective

141. (A) This policy has been extended to at least 60 days
(B) Nevertheless, I am asking you to kindly make an exception
(C) Please add a credit to my account to be used for future purchases
(D) I sent the package back to you two weeks after I received it

142. (A) be selling
(B) having been sold
(C) are sold
(D) will sell

GO ON TO THE NEXT PAGE.

From:	Tony Norman <tnorman@creativeaim.com>
To:	Annie Baker <abaker@fanmail.com>
Re:	Incentive program
Date:	June 5

Hi Annie,

I'm so pleased that I got to meet with you in Miami. At dinner, you mentioned the customer incentive program you ran last year. You said the program ------- a contest that monitored customer feedback, with
      143.
prizes for the employees receiving the most positive responses. I was impressed with how the program improved ------- and morale. It sounds
                                                  144.
------- the best way to let employees know how much their contributions
145.
are valued. -------. Would you be able to talk with me about how you
        146.
monitored feedback and the types of prizes you offered?

I look forward to hearing from you.

Sincerely,
Tony

143. (A) will involve
(B) to involve
(C) involving
(D) involved

144. (A) necessity
(B) productivity
(C) expenses
(D) preference

145. (A) as if
(B) instead of
(C) about
(D) like

146. (A) I would be happy to work on the sales presentation
(B) I canceled the meeting with our colleagues
(C) I would like to do something similar at my company
(D) I plan to hire additional representatives

Directions: In this part you will read a selection of texts, such as magazine and newspaper articles, e-mails, and instant messages. Each text or set of texts is followed by several questions. Select the best answer for each question and mark the letter (A), (B), (C), or (D) on your answer sheet.

Questions 147-148 refer to the following notice.

NOTICE – MOCA TENANTS AND VISITORS!

The sidewalk along Foothills Parkway is scheduled to be repaired next week. Due to safety concerns, the main entrance of the Museum of Contemporary Art (MOCA) will be inaccessible from Monday, December 19 through Friday, December 23.

MOCA tenants and visitors are advised to use the south entrance on Colorado Avenue. To get to the reception desk on the second floor, take either the escalator or the elevator, both of which can be found at the south entrance of the building.

147. What is the purpose of the notice?
  (A) To introduce changes to certain security measures.
  (B) To announce the temporary closure of an entryway.
  (C) To report the vacancy of a property.
  (D) To disclose the new location of a company.

148. What is suggested about MOCA?
  (A) Many people live there.
  (B) It will reopen on Friday.
  (C) The main entrance is on Foothills Parkway.
  (D) The renovation project will take one month.

GO ON TO THE NEXT PAGE.

From:	Jamie Keltner, Project Manager
To:	Corporate Resource Team
Re:	Overseas Support
Date:	October 10

Hi Team,

At next week's strategy session, we will address the specific needs of our company representatives working at our new overseas retail locations. Our goal is to have each employee fully trained in marketing our products and in client retention. I'm requesting that each of you be ready to present two ideas on the best ways to provide them with training and logistical support at levels comparable to their domestic counterparts.

Thanks,

Jamie Keltner

Team Lead, Echoplex Instruments

149. According to the e-mail, what is true about Echoplex Instruments?
(A) It markets symphonic instruments.
(B) It has an international presence.
(C) It plans to open several more stores.
(D) It just produced a new line of products.

150. What does Mr. Keltner ask employees to do?
(A) Accept overseas deployment.
(B) Contact clients.
(C) Attend a training session.
(D) Prepare for a meeting.

Read This First - Important Information!

At Colby-Sanford Inc., our reputation is based on our high-quality, easy-to-assemble cabinets, and we guarantee total satisfaction with your purchase.

Prior to assembling your Colby-Sanford product, check the parts list to make sure that all parts have been included in the box.

If your item is missing any parts, for instance, assembly hardware, or if it has been damaged during shipping, DO NOT return the product to the retail location from which you purchased it; retailers are only vendors and do not carry replacement parts. Instead, contact us directly, and we will send you the item(s) required free of charge. You can reach us by:

- visiting us at www.Colby-Sanford.com to order replacement parts online;

- sending us an e-mail at parts@Colby-Sanford.com; or

- calling us anytime at 202-767-1111

151. What is the purpose of the information?
 (A) To offer incentives to loyal Colby-Sanford vendors.
 (B) To direct customers to nearby retail locations.
 (C) To inform customers where to obtain product assembly.
 (D) To notify customers how to resolve a problem involving their purchase.

152. What is suggested about Colby-Sanford, Inc.?
 (A) It recommends returning damaged goods to the retailers.
 (B) It has a new assembly hardware system.
 (C) It supplies a product catalog with each order.
 (D) It has customer service representatives available at all times.

GO ON TO THE NEXT PAGE.

Maria Cicero [8:01 A.M.]

Hey Lance. I'm at the restaurant. I need to start doing prep work for the wedding reception this afternoon. But I don't have a key and the kitchen door is locked.

Lance Kudgel [8:03 A.M.]

Chef Poncey isn't there? He usually shows up early on the day of a big event.

Maria Cicero [8:05 A.M.]

Right? I'm confused. And the dishwashing crew isn't here, either. You'll be in this morning, won't you?

Lance Kudgel [8:07 A.M.]

Um, no. Actually, I'm on my way to a meeting at corporate headquarters, but I'll swing by and let you in. Give me 15 minutes.

Maria Cicero [8:08 A.M.]

OK. I'll wait in my car. I'm parked underground. Text me when you get here?

153. Who most likely is Mr. Kudgel?
(A) An anchorman.
(B) A restaurant manager.
(C) A bartender.
(D) An executive chef.

154. What does Ms. Cicero most likely mean when she writes, "I'm confused"?
(A) She received the wrong paperwork.
(B) She doesn't know where her key is.
(C) The band should be there already.
(D) The chef usually arrives early.

Visiting Portsmouth? These are must-see destinations!

Waterville Valley Resort

Enjoy hiking, backpacking and mountain bike trails that lead to backcountry areas of the surrounding White Mountain National Forest. A restaurant and swimming pool (both open in summer only) overlook the lake. Groceries, gifts and snacks can be purchased at the resort gift shop.

The River Casino and Sports Bar

On the Nashua River. A spectacular replica of the original Eiffel Tower in Paris. Open daily 10 a.m. – 10 p.m.; $15 admission includes souvenir program and elevator ride to observation deck.

George Washington House Museum

930 S. Westmoreland Blvd, ☎(479) 444-0066. The house Washington lived in while he taught at the University of New Hampshire. It has been turned into a small museum with a gift shop and a short tour. $5 adults, $1 kids.

The University of New Hampshire

The main campus, home of the Wildcats, is located at the west end of Dickson Street. "Track Capital of the World" and renowned center of NEC sports, the campus is situated atop one of the many hills in the town. Check out the many stadiums (football, baseball, track, gymnastics, basketball, soccer, etc.) and the many, varied academic buildings on campus. Also, the New Hampshire Union has a coffee shop and a movie theater, and the K.T. Mullins Library has free Internet access. Just ask the circulation desk.

155. What is purpose of the information?
   (A) To highlight the accomplishments of local athletes.
   (B) To give transportation information.
   (C) To describe notable landmarks.
   (D) To provide a schedule of event.

156. What is indicated about the K.T. Mullins Library?
   (A) It is closed on Monday.
   (B) It is located inside the Washington House Museum.
   (C) It features sporting events.
   (D) It offers free Internet access.

157. According to the information, what do the Eiffel Tower replica and the Washington House Museum have in common?
   (A) Both are located in the White Mountain National Forest.
   (B) Both display historical artifacts.
   (C) Both offer guided tours.
   (D) Both charge a small admission fee.

GO ON TO THE NEXT PAGE.

FIRST AMERICAN MILWAUKEE EXEC RECEIVES AWARD

BY LOU DOBBS

WAUKESHA – The Wisconsin Land Title Association (WLTA), one of the state's oldest trade associations, presented Ronald Reich, a Vice President and the State Agency Manager for First American Title Insurance Company, with the esteemed Title Person of the Year Award during the WLTA Annual Conference and Business Meeting in Waukesha, July 20.

The award, which is the highest honor bestowed by WLTA, recognizes significant and long-time contributions to the title industry and the association.

"Ronald has been a constant champion for our association and the title industry in Wisconsin, and we are honored to present him with this prestigious award," said Lou Souza, Executive Vice President and CEO of WLTA. "The contributions he has made as part of our association leadership are too many to name, and we are privileged to have him among our ranks."

Reich has been an active WLTA member for a number of years, serving on numerous committees as both a member and chairman. He served as WLTA president (2009-2010) and currently serves as a trustee of the WLTA Political Action Committee and co-chairs the WLTA PAC Fundraising Group.

Reich works out of First American's Milwaukee office and has been with the company for 16 years. In his 29- year title insurance career, most of his time has been devoted to working with independent agents as an agency manager. He managed an agency for three years in Milwaukee.

Before he entered the title industry, Reich spent four years with Sturgeon & Wimbley, where at the age of 24, he was one of their youngest sales managers ever.

Reich earned a Bachelor of Science degree in business administration from the University of Texas and enjoys spending his free time with his wife, Leah, and their four children.

158. What is most likely true about Mr. Reich?
(A) He led efforts to simplify the title process.
(B) He designed a new type of insurance.
(C) He served on a WLTA committee.
(D) He has received several awards from the WLTA.

159. What was Mr. Reich's job at Sturgeon & Wimbley?
(A) Sales manager.
(B) Company spokesperson.
(C) Construction manager.
(D) Building supervisor.

160. What happened 16 years ago?
(A) Mr. Reich moved to Waukesha.
(B) Mr. Reich began working at First American Title Insurance Company.
(C) The WLTA revised its membership requirements.
(D) The WLTA first presented its award.

PUBLIC NOTICE

Utility Construction Scheduled for Martha Swann Park

MARCH 15 - As part of the Basement Flooding Protection Program, the City of Jacksonville will be modifying and upgrading the combined sewer system by implementing an underground storage tank in Martha Swann Park.

A diversion chamber will be constructed at the intersection of Napoleon Avenue and Spencer Avenue. These will also be sewer upgrades on Walker Boulevard between French Street and the park as part of this project. A map of the construction area can be accessed at:

http://www.cityplanning.gov/jacksonville_sewer

Construction is expected to begin Monday, April 6 and be completed in one year. Your co-operation and patience during the construction period is appreciated.

Important Advisory

Many people have landscaping, fences, irrigation systems or other physical features in front of their home which are within the City property limits. These may be in the way of the construction. In such cases, residents are advised to remove these items prior to the beginning of construction in order to avoid unnecessary damage. The City will not be responsible for damage to any privately-owned items installed on the City's property.

City of Jacksonville Department of Public Works

---

161. What is indicated about the construction project?
(A) It will cause flight delays.
(B) It will result in better access to the park.
(C) It will take place over a period of one year.
(D) It will include emergency repairs.

162. When will the roadwork initially begin?
(A) On a Monday.
(B) On a Friday.
(C) On a Saturday.
(D) On a Sunday.

163. What action does the City recommend?
(A) Taking public transportation.
(B) Avoiding driving during peak hours.
(C) Using the west entrance to Martha Swann Park.
(D) Removing items from City property.

GO ON TO THE NEXT PAGE.

Sea Pines is Back on the Map!

SEA PINES (January 24) – According to a year-end study conducted by the Atlantic Coast Hospitality Index, tourism at our beaches improved dramatically this last summer, and the hotel industry showed greater profits this year than last. Hotel occupancy averaged 102 percent during the peak summer months. This was a big increase from last summer's average of just 77 percent. –[1]–

Last spring, Sea Pines saw the opening of the area's largest hotel, The Regal Palms Resort and Casino. The new resort was at full capacity nearly every weekend during the summer. Weekday occupancy also surpassed expectations. –[2]–

The hotel's manager Savannah Richards said, "Tourists were thrilled with the array of amenities offered, including 24-hour dining options, a free shuttle between casinos, and great value for their money. In fact, many have already reserved rooms for next summer. –[3]–

Sea Pines has become the most popular tourist destination in the region, with about 15 percent more beachgoers than Myrtle Beach, its biggest competitor. –[4]–

Tourists continue to visit the area after the prime summer months, keeping hotel rooms occupied longer.

164. What is the purpose of the article?

(A) To discuss job opportunities in the hotel industry.

(B) To compare the economies of two neighboring cities.

(C) To announce the opening of a new hotel.

(D) To provide information about the local tourism industry.

165. What is suggested about The Regal Palms Resort and Casino?

(A) It has contributed to the rise in tourism.

(B) It has forced smaller hotels to close.

(C) It attracts a criminal element.

(D) It will expand to Myrtle Beach.

166. What is NOT indicated about Sea Pines?

(A) Its beach is more popular than Myrtle Beach.

(B) Its new hotel employs Ms. Richards.

(C) It offers good value for consumers.

(D) It recently held a beach cleanup weekend.

167. In which of the positions marked [1], [2], [3], and [4] does the following sentence best belong?

"Experts attribute this to the increasing number of casinos in the area, overall lower prices, and an abundance of new restaurants, hotels, and attractions."

(A) [1].

(B) [2].

(C) [3].

(D) [4].

GO ON TO THE NEXT PAGE.

From:	Karen Claibourne
To:	All Employees
Re:	Convention
Date:	May 4

✉ Proposal.doc 23.0 KB

Hey guys and gals!

The 10th annual Great Midwestern Sales and Marketing Convention (GMSMC) will take place from June 9-12 here in Louisville. Convention organizers have asked local e-commerce specialists to contribute by giving a keynote speech, leading a seminar, or working in the exhibition hall. ---[1]---.

Our chief executive officer, Sanjit Darvish, wants us to take advantage of this excellent opportunity for Darvish Concepts to achieve visibility on a national stage. It is sure to help us to expand our client base. Mr. Darvish has already agreed to give a keynote speech about using survey results to create successful e-commerce marketing campaigns. ---[2]---.

I am organizing our company's booth for the exhibition hall. If you would like to help, please come to Room C556 at 2:00 P.M. next Monday, May 11, for a planning meeting. ---[3]---.

If you would like to lead a seminar, please complete the attached proposal form and return it to me by May 18. This will help me ensure that none of our seminar topics overlap. ---[4]---. Seminar ideas will be discussed and approved at a manager's meeting on May 25.

168. What is the purpose of the e-mail?

(A) To apologize for missing a deadline.

(B) To invite staff to submit an application.

(C) To request responses to a marketing survey.

(D) To remind staff to apply for travel reimbursement.

169. What is suggested about Darvish Concepts?

(A) It is hosting the GMSMC.

(B) It is located in Louisville.

(C) It has been in business for ten years.

(D) It serves clients throughout Kentucky.

170. According to the e-mail, why does Mr. Darvish want employees to participate in the GMSMC?

(A) So they can attract new clients.

(B) So they can listen to his keynote speech.

(C) So they can learn new marketing strategies.

(D) So they can share the results of the survey.

171. In which of the positions marked [1], [2], [3], and [4] does the following sentence best belong?

"You may present alone or with a partner."

(A) [1].

(B) [2].

(C) [3].

(D) [4].

GO ON TO THE NEXT PAGE.

Matt Pecora [9:05 A.M.]

Deandra, when we last spoke, production was nearly finished on the boxes and other packaging for Rothschild's. Where are we now?

Deandra Whiteside [9:06 A.M.]

The vacuum-seal bags, folding cartons and take-out boxes were supposed to arrive at Rothschild's warehouse on Monday, but the hurricane really messed up our delivery schedule.

Matt Pecora [9:07 A.M.]

Are they aware of this?

Tina Shultzer [9:08 A.M.]

They should be, but I was waiting to hear from the drivers. Dylan, what have you got?

Dylan Kubinski [9:09 A.M.]

I spoke with them early this morning. They're back on the road now, but they're separated. They should start arriving at Rothschild's warehouse sometime in the middle of the night. Not sure in what order though.

Tina Shultzer [9:11 A.M.]

Ok. I'll tell them to have someone on-hand to accept the delivery. How many pallets are we talking again?

Deandra Whiteside [9:12 A.M.]

24. As long as the truck containing the folding cartons gets there tonight, we should be in good shape.

Matt Pecora [9:13 A.M.]

The contract is for us to provide packaging materials for all of Rothschild's products, not just the smaller ones. Let's make sure we get everything to them ASAP. Tina, get someone on the phone and let them know for sure what's going on.

172. What type of business do the people most likely work for?
- (A) A restaurant supply company.
- (B) A trucking company.
- (C) A packaging manufacturer.
- (D) A food delivery service.

173. What problem are the people discussing?
- (A) An order was incorrect.
- (B) A driver did not report for work.
- (C) A shipment was delayed.
- (D) A warehouse was destroyed.

174. What will Ms. Shultzer most likely do next?
- (A) Call a driver.
- (B) Contact the client.
- (C) Cancel a shipment.
- (D) Place an order.

175. At 9:08 A.M., what does Ms. Shultzer most likely mean when she writes, "What have you got"?
- (A) She thinks Mr. Kubinski should deliver some boxes.
- (B) She needs Mr. Kubinski to drive to the warehouse.
- (C) She wants Mr. Kubinski to provide delivery information.
- (D) She expects Mr. Kubinski to pay the drivers.

GO ON TO THE NEXT PAGE.

From:	Martin Dietrich
To:	All Foursquare Design employees
Re:	July Renovations
Date:	May 23

✉ Schedule.xls (121.7 KB)

As most of you are aware, our schedule will be somewhat disrupted during the first week of July. Various rooms and offices will need to be vacated for certain periods to allow work crews to repaint, replace old furniture, and install new carpeting.

Affected employees will need to box up all their office items by 5:00 p.m. on the day before their room is scheduled for work (please see the attached schedule). Two teams of workers will be on-site, so more than one room at a time will need to be vacated. Note that any rooms due for work on Monday must be packed up and vacated by Friday afternoon, June 29.

Boxes will be provided. Leave your boxes in the rooms for the work crews to remove. Please label them with your name and office number so that the crews can return them to the correct offices once the work is complete. Please make arrangements to continue working on your assignments while the work crews are in your rooms. Conference Room C will remain available to be used as a workspace for the entire week. Another possible option is to request permission from your supervisor to telecommute for one or two days.

Please have patience with these temporary inconveniences and do not hesitate to contact me with any questions or concerns.

Martin Dietrich, Office Manager

FOURSQUARE Remodeling Schedule – July 2 to July 6

Date	Work Scheduled	Affected Employees
Monday, July 2	Office 1103	Al Spears Mickey Gorshak
Tuesday, July 3	Conference Room A	
Wednesday, July 4	Office 1108	Sandra Tonklin Luke Taylor
Thursday, July 5	Conference Room B	
Friday, July 6	Office 1101	Steve Chu Elliot Delaney Carmela Nastasia

176. Why was the memo sent to employees?
(A) To request feedback about new work facilities
(B) To address their complaints about building maintenance.
(C) To inform them of upcoming renovations.
(D) To announce that the firm will be relocating.

177. What are employees instructed to do?
(A) Submit expense reports.
(B) Schedule a meeting with their supervisors.
(C) Indicate which office supplies are theirs.
(D) Update their contact information online.

178. What is stated about Conference Room C?
(A) It will be renovated on July 6.
(B) It will be available for video conferencing.
(C) Employees may gather there for work.
(D) A scheduling meeting will be held there.

179. When should Ms. Tonklin be ready to vacate her office?
(A) On March 12.
(B) On March 27.
(C) On July 3.
(D) On July 4.

180. What is suggested about Mr. Delaney?
(A) He is the head of a department.
(B) He requested the use of a conference room.
(C) He shares an office with colleagues.
(D) He will work off-site on July 5.

GO ON TO THE NEXT PAGE.

WESTFIELD FOOD COOPERATIVE FARM SHARE PROGRAM

You're Welcome to Join Us!

Westfield Food Cooperative invites you to participate in its community-supported Farm Share program. Members enjoy fresh farm produce during our growing season from April to November.

Members receive a farm share once a week. A full-size share is $675, and a half-size share is $350. Half-size shareholders receive half of the full-sized share of produce each week.

Our farm produce is locally-grown without the use of pesticides and herbicides. All producers are Certified Organic.

For more information or to sign up for a share, please visit our Web site, www.westfieldfood.org

Join Farm Share and receive the following benefits:

Lifetime membership to the Westfield Food Cooperative, giving you direct access to local growers and vendors

More than 25 varieties of in-season vegetables, fruits, and herbs, harvested by local producers and delivered fresh to your home by our staff

A selection of pick-your-own citrus fruits, bananas and avocados, and other fruits

Access to our member Web site with updates and a Farm Share newsletter

Discounts on events at the Co-Op for the annual summer music festival. Events cost $15, but members pay $10

WESTFIELD FOOD COOPERATIVE FARM SHARE
REGISTRATION FORM

MEMBER INFORMATION		
Name: Kenneth Dolan		
Address: 30048 Arapahoe Drive, Westfield, CO 80032		
Membership plan:	⦿	Full share
	○	Half share
Please provide the names of other individuals in your household. These are the only other individuals who will be permitted to sign for your weekly share:		
Lois Dolan, William Dolan		
Preferred Delivery Date:	○	Thursday
	○	Friday

CLICK **HERE** TO SUBMIT PAYMENT

---

181. What is the purpose of the flyer?
(A) To invite people to a music festival.
(B) To promote a new product.
(C) To recruit summer interns.
(D) To advertise a farm program.

182. What is suggested about the workers at Westfield Food Co-op?
(A) They update the farm's Web site once a week.
(B) They create meals using the farm's products.
(C) They sell farm products at several local markets.
(D) They deliver farm produce from April to November.

183. What is NOT indicated about Westfield Food Co-op?
(A) It publishes a newsletter.
(B) It uses natural fertilizers.
(C) It hosts musical performances.
(D) It offers cooking classes.

184. What is true about Mr. Wentworth's membership?
(A) He must pick up his produce on Fridays.
(B) He is the only person who may pick up fruit.
(C) He is allowed to pick some of his fruit.
(D) He will be able to plant and grow his own vegetables.

185. How much should Mr. Wentworth pay for the membership?
(A) $10.
(B) $15.
(C) $350.
(D) $675.

GO ON TO THE NEXT PAGE.

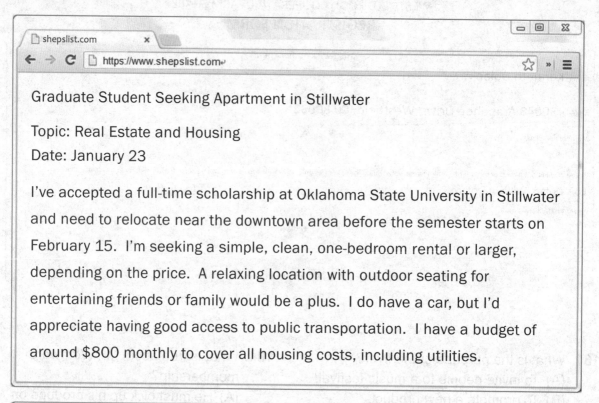

shepslist.com   ×

← → C   https://www.shepslist.com↵

Graduate Student Seeking Apartment in Stillwater

Topic: Real Estate and Housing
Date: January 23

I've accepted a full-time scholarship at Oklahoma State University in Stillwater and need to relocate near the downtown area before the semester starts on February 15. I'm seeking a simple, clean, one-bedroom rental or larger, depending on the price. A relaxing location with outdoor seating for entertaining friends or family would be a plus. I do have a car, but I'd appreciate having good access to public transportation. I have a budget of around $800 monthly to cover all housing costs, including utilities.

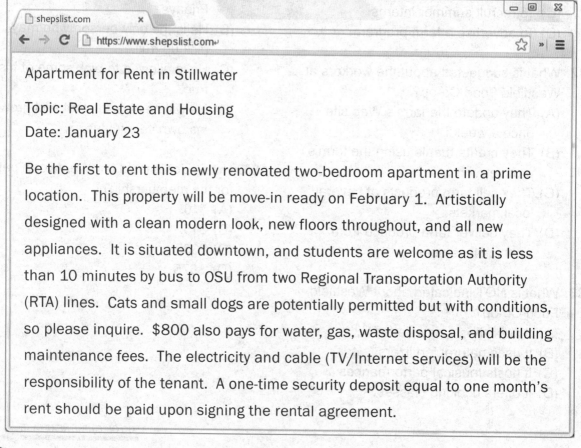

shepslist.com   ×

← → C   https://www.shepslist.com↵

Apartment for Rent in Stillwater

Topic: Real Estate and Housing
Date: January 23

Be the first to rent this newly renovated two-bedroom apartment in a prime location. This property will be move-in ready on February 1. Artistically designed with a clean modern look, new floors throughout, and all new appliances. It is situated downtown, and students are welcome as it is less than 10 minutes by bus to OSU from two Regional Transportation Authority (RTA) lines. Cats and small dogs are potentially permitted but with conditions, so please inquire. $800 also pays for water, gas, waste disposal, and building maintenance fees. The electricity and cable (TV/Internet services) will be the responsibility of the tenant. A one-time security deposit equal to one month's rent should be paid upon signing the rental agreement.

TO	Christine Coolidge <coolidgerental@waymail.com>
FROM	Dick Stilton <r_ctilton@mahal.com>
DATE	Apartment
SUBJECT	January 24

Dear Ms. Coolidge,

I noticed your rental listings on the Shep's List Web site. From the description, it sounds as if it may be just what I've been looking for. I'm eager to look at the apartment, and as luck will have it I'll be in Stillwater through Sunday, January 30. If I like the place and we agree to lease terms, I'd want to move in the same day that it's expected to be available. Actually, the timing couldn't be better! I hope to hear from you soon.

Thank you.

Dick Stilton
(802) 555-0122

186. Why is Mr. Stilton relocating?
  (A) To start a new job.
  (B) To return to his hometown.
  (C) To study full-time.
  (D) To take care of a family member.

187. Which cost would NOT be included in Mr. Stilton's rental agreement?
  (A) Water.
  (B) Electricity.
  (C) Gas.
  (D) Waste removal.

188. When does Mr. Stilton want to start living in the residence?
  (A) January 24.
  (B) January 30.
  (C) February 1.
  (D) February 15.

189. Why does Mr. Stilton send the e-mail?
  (A) To agree to the terms of the contract.
  (B) To change the details of a scholarship application.
  (C) To inquire about the availability of campus services.
  (D) To make an arrangement to view the property.

190. For what situation does Ms. Coolidge mention that she will need additional information?
  (A) When changes to the décor are needed.
  (B) When a tenant is ready to pay a security deposit.
  (C) When an apartment needs to be repaired.
  (D) When someone wants to keep an indoor pet.

GO ON TO THE NEXT PAGE.

American
Kitchen
Club

Professional equipment at wholesale prices

Hobart AM15-1
Electric High Temp Door-Type Dishwasher

You will never need to buy another dishwasher! Our best-selling model, the AM15-1, is made of easy-to-clean stainless steel and is operated by solid-state controls with digital displays.

Features: The unique door type and hot water/chemical sanitizing design make this professional-grade appliance ideal for busy restaurants of all sizes. Washes up to 56 racks per hour.

Warranty: We include a seven-year warranty on all parts and labor—an assurance to you that our dishwasher will last a long time.

REGULAR PURCHASE PRICE: $10,019.95

UKC MEMBERS: $9,299.95

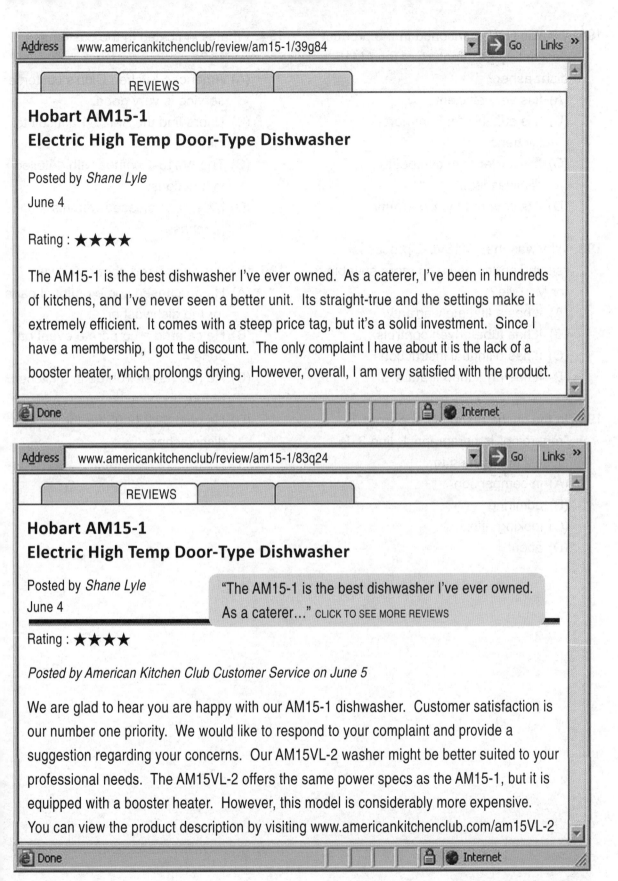

Address www.americankitchenclub/review/am15-1/39g84 ▾ → Go Links »

REVIEWS

Hobart AM15-1
Electric High Temp Door-Type Dishwasher

Posted by *Shane Lyle*

June 4

Rating : ★★★★

The AM15-1 is the best dishwasher I've ever owned. As a caterer, I've been in hundreds of kitchens, and I've never seen a better unit. Its straight-true and the settings make it extremely efficient. It comes with a steep price tag, but it's a solid investment. Since I have a membership, I got the discount. The only complaint I have about it is the lack of a booster heater, which prolongs drying. However, overall, I am very satisfied with the product.

Done 🔒 🌐 Internet

Address www.americankitchenclub/review/am15-1/83q24 ▾ → Go Links »

REVIEWS

Hobart AM15-1
Electric High Temp Door-Type Dishwasher

Posted by *Shane Lyle*

June 4

"The AM15-1 is the best dishwasher I've ever owned. As a caterer..." CLICK TO SEE MORE REVIEWS

Rating : ★★★★

Posted by American Kitchen Club Customer Service on June 5

We are glad to hear you are happy with our AM15-1 dishwasher. Customer satisfaction is our number one priority. We would like to respond to your complaint and provide a suggestion regarding your concerns. Our AM15VL-2 washer might be better suited to your professional needs. The AM15VL-2 offers the same power specs as the AM15-1, but it is equipped with a booster heater. However, this model is considerably more expensive. You can view the product description by visiting www.americankitchenclub.com/am15VL-2

Done 🔒 🌐 Internet

GO ON TO THE NEXT PAGE.➤

191. What is NOT mentioned in the product description as a feature of the AM15-1 dishwasher?

(A) It is very efficient.

(B) It is suitable for commercial kitchens.

(C) It is larger than competitors' dishwashers.

(D) It is covered by a warranty.

192. Why was the AM15VL-2 processor recommended as being more suitable for Mr. Lyle?

(A) It has a lifetime warranty.

(B) It has tube-driven controls.

(C) It has bilingual instructions.

(D) It has an added feature.

193. In the online response, the word "regarding" in paragraph 1, line 3, is closest in meaning to

(A) in comparison.

(B) admiring.

(C) looking after.

(D) about.

194. What is indicated in the customer review?

(A) American Kitchen Club's customer service is very good.

(B) Users find the AM15-1 difficult to clean.

(C) The AM15-1 comes with detailed instructions.

(D) Mr. Lyle is pleased with his purchase.

195. What is suggested about Mr. Lyle?

(A) He purchased some optional parts for the dishwasher.

(B) He catered a corporate event on June 4.

(C) He has never worked in a kitchen before.

(D) He paid $9,299.95 for the dishwasher.

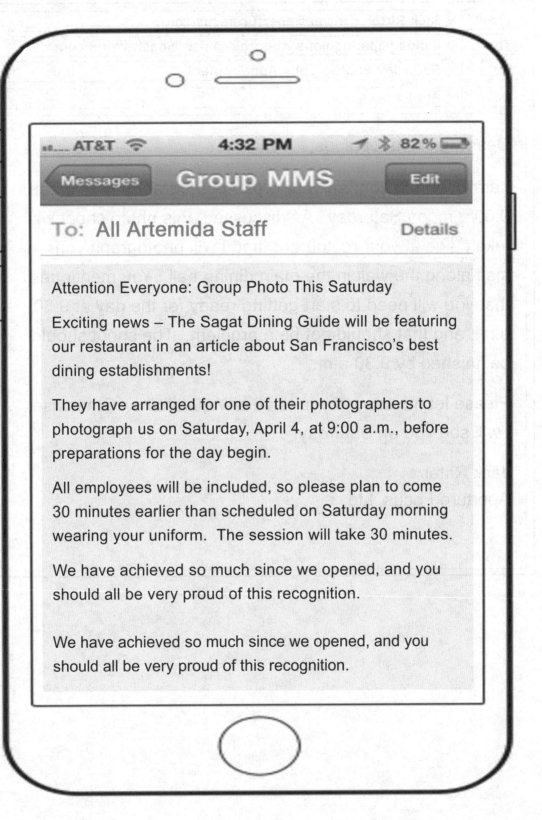

To: All Artemida Staff

Attention Everyone: Group Photo This Saturday

Exciting news – The Sagat Dining Guide will be featuring our restaurant in an article about San Francisco's best dining establishments!

They have arranged for one of their photographers to photograph us on Saturday, April 4, at 9:00 a.m., before preparations for the day begin.

All employees will be included, so please plan to come 30 minutes earlier than scheduled on Saturday morning wearing your uniform. The session will take 30 minutes.

We have achieved so much since we opened, and you should all be very proud of this recognition.

We have achieved so much since we opened, and you should all be very proud of this recognition.

GO ON TO THE NEXT PAGE.

From:	Jack Ritter <jritter@aperturefocus.com>
To:	Panos Papadopolous <georgio@artemidastaverna.com>
Re:	Saturday Photography Appointment
Date:	April 1

Dear Mr. Papadopolous,

I am writing to confirm your group photography session at 9:00 a.m. on Saturday. As discussed, this photo shoot will take place at your restaurant, and I will photograph your staff along the wall in the main dining hall. You mentioned that you will need to start getting ready for the day at 9:30 a.m., and that should not be a problem. The shoot should be finished by 9:30 a.m.

Please let me know if you have any questions. Otherwise I will see you on Saturday!

Jack Ritter
Aperture Focus, Ltd.

Greek Taverna Delights Potrero Hill

By Noah Pitnik, Staff Writer

Enter Artemida Taverna any day for lunch or dinner, and you'll hear the sound of bouzouki music. "That's the sound of my hometown, Artemida," says Panos Papadopolous, the restaurant's owner.

Opened two years ago, the Taverna has exceeded expectations. The menu features traditional Greek dishes prepared by chef Voula Markopoulo. She notes, "Our menus feature recipes passed down from one generation to the next." Offering a fresh serving of *spanikopita*, a savory spinach pastry, Markopoulo says, "This is exactly the way it would be served in Panos' home."

On a recent Wednesday afternoon, Yiannis Katsaros, a visitor from Athens, Greece, was dining at the Taverna. "I can't get over the authenticity of the flavors!" exclaimed Mr. Katsaros. "It's like the chef has taken me back to the old country and I'm dining at my nana's table."

Artemida Taverna is located at 23 DeHaro Street in Potrero Hill, and is open Monday through Saturday from 11:30 a.m. to 10:00 p.m. The interior is painted in the familiar Greek shades of blue and white reminiscent of the ocean, with a rotating gallery of artwork adorning the walls. The staff is friendly and the delicious food is reasonably priced.

Reservations are not required.

Artemida Taverna, 23 DeHaro Street, Potrero Hill, S.F. Hours: Mon.- Sat. 11:30 a.m. to 10:00 p.m. All major credit cards accepted. (415) 504-3210

GO ON TO THE NEXT PAGE.

196. Who most likely posted the notice?
- (A) Mr. Ritter.
- (B) Mr. Papadopolous.
- (C) Ms. Markopoulo
- (D) Mr. Pitnik.

197. What are employees instructed to do on April 4?
- (A) Arrive earlier than usual.
- (B) Work later than usual.
- (C) Be interviewed for a newspaper article.
- (D) Discuss locations for a holiday party.

198. What is true about the Artemida Taverna?
- (A) It is open every day for lunch.
- (B) It has recently changed ownership.
- (C) It features Greek cuisine.
- (D) It revises the menu seasonally.

199. What is indicated about the staff?
- (A) They have been featured in The Sagat Dining Guide more than once.
- (B) They will be photographed in the main dining room.
- (C) They take turns working the morning shift.
- (D) They wear brightly colored uniforms.

200. What does Mr. Katsaros say about the food?
- (A) He is disappointed with the portions.
- (B) He is surprised by the flavors.
- (C) He saw it featured in a magazine.
- (D) He thought it was reasonably priced.

Stop! This is the end of the test. If you finish before time is called, you may go back to Parts 5, 6, and 7 and check your work.

New TOEIC Listening Script

PART 1

1. (　　) (A) The men are fighting.
   (B) The men are dancing.
   (C) The men are eating.
   (D) The men are reading.

2. (　　) (A) The man is installing a window.
   (B) The woman is writing a note.
   (C) The boy is throwing a ball.
   (D) The girl is opening the door.

3. (　　) (A) Some people are swimming in a pool.
   (B) Some people are at the bus stop.
   (C) Some people are watching a parade.
   (D) Some people are at the zoo.

4. (　　) (A) The cafeteria is not crowded.
   (B) The library is closed.
   (C) The restaurant is being remodeled.
   (D) The stadium is being torn down.

5. (　　) (A) The woman is preparing some food.
   (B) They are in a theater.
   (C) They are on an airplane.
   (D) The man is giving a presentation.

6. (　　) (A) They are working on an assembly line.
   (B) They are playing in a sandbox.
   (C) They are helping set up a party.
   (D) They are not wearing protective clothing.

GO ON TO THE NEXT PAGE.

PART 2

7. (   ) What time is the board meeting?
    (A) In the main conference room.
    (B) Her name is Susanne.
    (C) It starts at 1:30.

8. (   ) Where should I put these samples for the sales presentation?
    (A) Almost everyone signed up.
    (B) On the table by the door.
    (C) Just coffee, tea, and some pastries.

9. (   ) Why did you return your new laptop?
    (A) It's cold this morning.
    (B) Because the screen was slightly cracked.
    (C) A shop in the mall.

10. (   ) Would you care for a beverage?
    (A) $500 each.
    (B) A glass of sparkling water, please.
    (C) I can't do it today.

11. (   ) When are you leaving for Vancouver?
    (A) On Tuesday night.
    (B) If I have time.
    (C) Near the entrance to the theater.

12. (   ) How much do you pay for your Internet service?
    (A) Not very often.
    (B) Sure, you can use it.
    (C) $79.95 per month.

13. (   ) What should I include in my research proposal?
    (A) Because I was out of town.
    (B) No, we haven't found one yet.
    (C) I know Dan's written a lot of them.

14. (   ) Have you met Mr. Swisher, the new director of sales?
    (A) Oh, we used to work together.
    (B) At the board meeting next Monday.
    (C) The sales department.

15. (　　) Do you need any assistance filling out the registration form?

    (A) Have you been checked-in?

    (B) No, it appears to be straightforward.

    (C) These seats are empty.

16. (　　) How did you like the café?

    (A) No, only on special occasions.

    (B) You were right. It wasn't crowded.

    (C) Around the corner from the office.

17. (　　) Was it Bob or Charlie who reviewed the customer surveys?

    (A) Open a customer account.

    (B) You know, I'm not really sure.

    (C) It is a 20-minute walk from here.

18. (　　) You'll be at the reception dinner, won't you?

    (A) In tomorrow's newspaper.

    (B) Yes, but I might be a little late.

    (C) I was disappointed with it.

19. (　　) Which room is Mr. Ball staying in at the hotel?

    (A) On Sedgwick Avenue.

    (B) I'll stay for another hour.

    (C) We can ask at the front desk.

20. (　　) Will our catering staff be wearing special uniforms?

    (A) Oh, it's a bit too large.

    (B) Thanks, but we have plenty of help.

    (C) Yes, I ordered them today.

21. (　　) Do you want this sent by regular mail, or do you want express delivery?

    (A) No, this is the wrong address.

    (B) Sign on the line here.

    (C) Regular mail, please.

22. (　　) Would you be interested in giving a lecture at the seminar?

    (A) When is it being held again?

    (B) I enjoyed meeting her very much.

    (C) I think you should speak with the client.

GO ON TO THE NEXT PAGE.

23. (   ) The automated sealing machine was repaired yesterday, wasn't it?
      (A) Yes, I have one of those.
      (B) No, it'll be done tomorrow.
      (C) We just received several large orders.

24. (   ) Who'll be the host of the awards banquet?
      (A) Ms. Leiberman from the nominating committee.
      (B) I believe it's been postponed to next week.
      (C) You don't think we need a bigger video screen?

25. (   ) Mr. Evans, I'm having problems printing the report.
      (A) I wasn't there.
      (B) You can just email it to me.
      (C) It's straight down the hall.

26. (   ) The snacks and drinks are complimentary on the flight, right?
      (A) Do you prefer an aisle seat?
      (B) Run the credit card again, please.
      (C) Only in business class.

27. (   ) Who's going to be the new manager of product development?
      (A) I can't wait to see your new apartment.
      (B) It's in the basement.
      (C) They're still interviewing candidates.

28. (   ) Ms. Klein wants us to complete the inventory by the end of our shift.
      (A) I have a dentist's appointment at noon today.
      (B) I am looking forward it.
      (C) No, my subscription's expired.

29. (   ) Weren't the windows of the building cleaned over the weekend?
      (A) Probably just read a book.
      (B) The nearby movie theater.
      (C) It rained last night.

30. (   ) Does anyone have time to help me unload the delivery truck?
      (A) Larry just finished his break.
      (B) Only once or twice.
      (C) Look in the bottom drawer.

31. (   ) We need to recruit experienced telemarketers to sell this product.
    (A) Maybe we should offer training.
    (B) Yes, he called earlier this morning.
    (C) It'll pass inspection, no problem.

PART 3

Questions 32 through 34 refer to the following conversation.

M : Hi, I just bought a house with some land and I'm interested in growing some vegetables. So I need to buy some seeds. I have a question though. Could you give me some advice about what grows best in our region?

W : Actually, the best way for you to get started will be one of our store's gardening classes. There is a new beginner series starting this Wednesday night. It meets once a week for three weeks.

M : I'd be interested in that, but I know the basics of gardening. I just moved here so I'm unfamiliar with such a dry climate. My needs are a bit specific.

W : Yes, on second thought, maybe the beginner's class is going to be a little too simple for you. Here is a list of all the classes we offer at the garden center. Perhaps the intermediate series is a better fit. If you follow me, I'll show you our selection of seeds and bulbs.

32. (   ) What is the man interested in doing?
    (A) Teaching a class.
    (B) Contacting a landscape designer.
    (C) Starting a vegetable garden.
    (D) Purchasing gardening tools.

33. (   ) What does the woman suggest?
    (A) Using a Web site.
    (B) Visiting a different store.
    (C) Purchasing a book.
    (D) Attending a class.

34. (   ) What does the woman give the man?
    (A) A list of courses.
    (B) A textbook.
    (C) Free samples.
    (D) Contact information.

GO ON TO THE NEXT PAGE.

Questions 35 through 37 *refer to the following conversation.*

W : Thomas, I wanted to talk to you about your sales last month. I only sold half of my quota.

M : I didn't meet my monthly sales goals either. Ever since Flash Mobile started offering unlimited data plans, fewer customers are willing to sign up with us.

W : Management should offer incentives to attract more customers like free phones when you sign a two-year contract.

M : I agree. We have to figure out how we can compete in this market.

35. (   ) Who most likely are the speakers?
    (A) Manufacturing supervisors.
    (B) Automobile mechanics.
    (C) Advertising executives.
    (D) Mobile phone service plan salespeople.

36. (   ) What problem are the speakers discussing?
    (A) Management directives have been inconsistent.
    (B) A business has been losing sales.
    (C) New products have received poor reviews.
    (D) The sales department is understaffed.

37. (   ) What solution does the woman suggest?
    (A) Soliciting customer feedback.
    (B) Advertising online.
    (C) Offering incentives to customers.
    (D) Hiring additional staff.

Questions 38 through 40 *refer to the following conversation.*

M : Good afternoon, Monica. I didn't see you at the talk about market valuation this morning. Did you just arrive at the conference?

W : Yes, my flight from Des Moines was delayed and I had a long wait in the taxi line at the airport. Anyway, how has the turnout been so far? I'll be presenting later this afternoon and want to make sure I have enough copies of my handout.

M : Attendance was moderate. I'd say about 150 people were there. Many of my associates won't be coming until tomorrow, when the heavy-hitters make their presentations. And from my experience, the afternoon sessions tend to be less crowded.

W : Thanks. That's good to know. I definitely don't need more handouts, so I can save the time and effort. See you later.

38. (　　) Why was the woman late?
　　　　(A) She had to wait for transportation.
　　　　(B) She was helping a colleague.
　　　　(C) She lost her conference badge.
　　　　(D) She went to the wrong location.

39. (　　) What does the woman ask about?
　　　　(A) Some equipment rentals.
　　　　(B) A registration procedure.
　　　　(C) Some changes to a schedule.
　　　　(D) The number of attendees.

40. (　　) What does the man say?
　　　　(A) The woman may need more fliers.
　　　　(B) The woman may have missed her session.
　　　　(C) Fewer people attend morning sessions.
　　　　(D) More people will attend tomorrow.

Questions 41 through 43 refer to the following conversation.

M : Hi, I ordered a ceramic tea set from your Web site, but when it arrived, some of the cups were broken. The delivery service must have dropped the package. It was clearly marked "fragile."

W : Oh, I'm sorry to hear that. However, it happens from time to time. Since your purchase was guaranteed, I can send you another set.

M : Well, I'd like to have it replaced as soon as possible, since I was planning to give it to someone as a gift next weekend.

W : All right, let me check our inventory on the computer to see if we have that exact tea set in stock.

41. (　　) Why is the man calling?
　　　　(A) A name is misspelled.
　　　　(B) A Web site is not working.
　　　　(C) A shipment is late.
　　　　(D) A product is damaged.

42. (　　) What does the man request?
　　　　(A) A tracking number.
　　　　(B) A refund.
　　　　(C) A replacement.
　　　　(D) A catalog.

GO ON TO THE NEXT PAGE.

43. (   ) What will the woman do next?
    (A) Check an inventory.
    (B) Call a warehouse.
    (C) Talk to her manager.
    (D) Set up an appointment.

Questions 44 through 46 *refer to the following conversation between three speakers.*

M : Hello, we're interested in these avocados. They're organic, aren't they?

Woman US : Yes, they are. In fact, these were grown by Dahlstrom Farms, which is just down the road from here.

Woman UK : Oh, so they're local as well as organic?

Woman US : Right.

M : Well, they look awesome. Give us two pounds, please.

Woman UK : That seems a bit much, dear. Aside from salads, what other uses do we have for two pounds of avocado?

Woman US : Oh, you could make guacamole! There are free recipe cards over there that you can take if you'd like.

44. (   ) Where is the conversation most likely taking place?
    (A) At a restaurant.
    (B) At a farmer's market.
    (C) At a flower shop.
    (D) At a tourist center.

45. (   ) According to the American woman, what is true about the product?
    (A) It is locally grown.
    (B) It is new this season.
    (C) It is currently discounted.
    (D) It is only available today.

46. (   ) What is the British woman concerned about?
    (A) Supporting local producers.
    (B) Freshness of salad ingredients.
    (C) Prices of avocados.
    (D) Uses for avocados.

Questions 47 through 49 *refer to the following conversation.*

W : I'd like to book a direct flight to Nashville on June 25th, please. Are there any flights that arrive in Nashville in the late afternoon?

M : Yes, there's a direct flight that will land in Nashville at 5:45 p.m.

W : Hmmm. That's cutting it a bit close. Is there anything earlier? I need time to set up some equipment for a 7:00 p.m. product demonstration.

M : In that case, your only option is to take a connecting flight through Indianapolis. If that's fine with you, there's a flight that will get you to Nashville earlier in the afternoon.

47. (   ) What is the woman inquiring about?
      (A) Extra baggage fees.
      (B) Flight arrival times.
      (C) Payment option.
      (D) A ticket upgrade.

48. (   ) What does the woman mean by "That's cutting it a bit close"?
      (A) She needs to be there earlier.
      (B) She wants more options.
      (C) She has already bought a ticket.
      (D) She is happy with the service she received.

49. (   ) What does the man recommend?
      (A) Using a credit card.
      (B) Speaking to a manager.
      (C) Purchasing some travel insurance.
      (D) Taking a different route.

Questions 50 through 52 _refer to the following conversation._

M : Hey, Paulina. I didn't return your phone call yesterday because I've been busy planning Ms. Walker's farewell party. It's hard to imagine her leaving us, isn't it?

W : It is. She's been the driving force of the company for how many years now?

M : Fifteen years as CEO. But listen, it's a surprise party, so don't spill the beans. Everyone will need to be in the main conference room before 5 o'clock on Friday to surprise her.

W : Um, that's a problem for me. I won't be there right at five. I have an appointment on the other side of town at four. But I will be sure to come as soon as I'm done.

50. (   ) What is the main topic of the conversation?
      (A) An executive's retirement.
      (B) A budget review.
      (C) A conference presentation.
      (D) A company relocation.

GO ON TO THE NEXT PAGE.

51. (   ) What does the man mean by "don't spill the beans"?
     (A) Arrive early at an event.
     (B) Keep some information secret.
     (C) Check an account.
     (D) Reserve a room.

52. (   ) What will the woman be doing at four o'clock on the day of the event?
     (A) Interviewing for a new job.
     (B) Meeting a client.
     (C) Completing a report.
     (D) Attending a party.

Questions 53 through 55 refer to the following conversation.

W : Hi, Dennis. It's Sue Taylor. I'm afraid I have some bad news. I'm calling to let you know that I've just missed my flight back to New York. So unfortunately, I'll have to spend another night here in Kansas City, which means I won't make it into the office tomorrow.

M : That's not good. The V.P. of sales is coming tomorrow morning and I was counting on you being here for this important meeting. Are you equipped for videoconferencing?

W : Well, there is a business center here in the hotel. But I'm not sure if it's equipped for videoconferencing. Let me go down there and see if the center has the necessary equipment.

53. (   ) What problem does the woman inform the man about?
     (A) She lost her computer.
     (B) Her luggage did not arrive.
     (C) Her password is incorrect.
     (D) She missed a flight.

54. (   ) What does the man suggest?
     (A) Joining a meeting by videoconference.
     (B) Returning to a hotel.
     (C) Consulting a travel agency.
     (D) Using a car service to visit a client.

55. (   ) What does the woman plan to do next?
     (A) Report a complaint.
     (B) Go to a repair shop.
     (C) Check for some equipment.
     (D) Call an airline.

M : Carol, let me pick your brain about the declining sales of our ceiling fans. The new sales report just came out and there's a dramatic decrease in the number of ceiling fans we sold.

W : Well, I have my suspicions, but... I think it could be related to the online customer reviews. A lot of people are complaining that do-it-yourself installation is very time-consuming and difficult despite the detailed instructions.

M : I bet you're right. What do you think about offering some kind of discount on installation? We have the manpower; it's just a matter of forming some kind of cohesive policy.

W : That's a great idea. I'll set up a meeting and we'll figure out how to do that.

56. (   ) What is the man concerned about?
- (A) A scheduling conflict.
- (B) A missing part.
- (C) Poor sales figures.
- (D) Repairing furniture.

57. (   ) What complaint do customers have?
- (A) A product is difficult to install.
- (B) A Web site is confusing.
- (C) Deliveries are late.
- (D) Selection is limited.

58. (   ) What does the man suggest doing?
- (A) Designing a survey.
- (B) Sending an e-mail.
- (C) Canceling an order.
- (D) Offering a discount.

Questions 59 through 61 _refer to the following conversation._

M : Hi, Ms. Sanchez, this is Steve Rossi from Ascendant Travel Agency. I'm calling to confirm that we'll meet as scheduled for our business lunch on Tuesday at your hotel chain's headquarters.

W : Of course, Steve. I'm looking forward to discussing the partnership between your travel agency and the hotel chain. There's a restaurant in the west annex of the hotel lobby called Christo's at the Plaza. I thought we could have lunch there. Okay?

M : That sounds great. By the way, where should I park?

W : You can use our parking garage next to the hotel. Bring the ticket to the front desk, and a receptionist will give you a parking pass. Just give it to the attendant on your way out.

GO ON TO THE NEXT PAGE.

59. (   ) Why did the man call Ms. Sanchez?
   (A) To book a hotel room.
   (B) To confirm an appointment.
   (C) To reschedule a meeting.
   (D) To make a dining reservation.

60. (   ) What is located in the west annex of the hotel?
   (A) A bank.
   (B) A restaurant.
   (C) A fitness center.
   (D) A concierge.

61. (   ) According to the woman, what can the man pick up at the front desk?
   (A) A parking pass.
   (B) A discount coupon.
   (C) Travel brochure.
   (D) A registration form.

Questions 62 through 64 *refer to the following conversation and graphic.*

M : Hello, Ms. Oliver. My name is Phil Bates and I'm calling from Allied Industries. We reviewed your job application and we'd like to interview you for the position of regional sales manager. Are you available on Friday at 2:00 p.m.?

W : Yes, I'm available on Friday afternoon. By the way, I have a question. I remember reading on the application form that candidates selected for an interview must provide at least three character references. Would you like those names now?

M : No, that's not necessary. We'll be sending you a follow-up email with details about the interview process shortly. I look forward to seeing you on Friday.

62. (   ) Why is the man calling?
   (A) To remind a customer.
   (B) To schedule an interview.
   (C) To request some sales.
   (D) To respond to a message.

63. (   ) What does the woman inquire about?
   (A) The cost of an item.
   (B) An application requirement.
   (C) An insurance policy.
   (D) The name of a company.

64. (   ) Look at the graphic. When should Jenna Oliver arrive at Allied Industries office?

(A) 2:10.

(B) 1:15.

(C) 1:50.

(D) 2:00.

From:	Phil Bates <p_bates@alliedindustries.com>
To:	Jenna Oliver <jenna74@heatmail.com>
Re:	Interview Process
Date:	December 15

Hi Jenna,

As I mentioned in our phone conversation, here are a few details about the interview process.

• Please arrive at our offices at least 10 minutes prior to your scheduled interview.
• Attire is business casual.
• Bring two copies of your updated resume.
• Print out a list of at least three (3) character references including the following information: (A) the person's name and full contact details (email, phone); (B) your relationship; (C) a short description of how long you've known this person.

See you on Friday.

Regards,
Phil Bates

Questions 65 through 67 refer to the following conversation and graphic.

W : Hello. Maybe you can help. My doctor recommended that I change my diet, starting with breakfast. He says I'm getting too much salt and not enough fiber. Do you have some sort of cereal that's high in fiber but low in sodium?

M : We have many different kinds of high fiber cereals. Here's my personal favorite, Honey Bran Flakes. It's really tasty!

W : Hmm. It sure has plenty of fiber but the salt content is too high. My doctor said I shouldn't have more than 20 milligrams of salt at breakfast.

M : How about this one, Hearty Bran? It's very low on salt, but it doesn't have a lot of flavor. You could, if you wanted, add your own fresh fruit.

GO ON TO THE NEXT PAGE.

65. (　　) Why is the woman looking for a certain product?
      (A) She wants to lose weight.
      (B) She has an allergy to certain foods.
      (C) She wants to eat healthy.
      (D) She has a favorite brand.

66. (　　) Look at the graphic. Which of the ingredients does the woman express concern about?
      (A) Sugar.
      (B) Fat.
      (C) Sodium.
      (D) Fiber.

Nutritional Information

Serving size: 250 grams

Calories 178

Amount per serving

Fat	7 grams
Protein	12 grams
Fiber	55 grams
Sodium	65 milligrams
Sugar	33 grams

67. (　　) What does the man suggest the woman do?
      (A) Try a free sample.
      (B) Go to a different store.
      (C) Buy a different item.
      (D) Speak with her doctor.

Questions 68 through 70 refer to the following conversation and coupon.

M : Excuse me, I want to replace the battery in my watch, but I only see lithium ion button cells and I need a silver oxide cell.

W : Oh, we're actually in the middle of reorganizing our selection of batteries to make it easier for customers to find what they need. The silver oxide batteries are over here for the moment. Follow me.

M : Great. I also have this discount coupon. It's good for silver oxide batteries, right?

W : Sure. Just present it to the cashier when paying for your purchases. Is there anything else I can help you find?

M : No, thanks.

68. (   ) What problem does the man mention?

    (A) He can't find an item.

    (B) He wants to return an item.

    (C) A product is defective.

    (D) A coupon has expired.

69. (   ) What does the woman say is currently happening?

    (A) New employees are being trained.

    (B) Merchandise is being relocated.

    (C) Watch batteries are being discontinued.

    (D) A major sale is being held.

70. (   ) Look at the graphic. What discount will the man most likely receive?

    (A) Buy one get one free.

    (B) 50%.

    (C) $3.

    (D) $5.

TIMEZONE ELECTRONICS | discount coupon

Batteries

Cylindrical $2 off
Non- Cylindrical alkaline $3 off
All other batteries $5 off

Redeemable at any participating TIMEZONE ELECTRONICS
Expires: November 30

timezone.com

PART 4

Questions 71 through 73 *refer to the following telephone message.*

This message is for Mr. Reynold Squire. This is Ava Nicks calling from the Oakland

Hills Library to let you know that the book you've requested, *The Head on the Door*,

has been returned and is now available. We'll hold it for you for two days, but feel free

to call if you need a little extra time. The number is 667-4455. And as a reminder, the

library is now observing winter hours, so we close an hour earlier each day at 8:30 p.m.

Thanks Mr. Squire, and have a nice day.

GO ON TO THE NEXT PAGE.

71. (   ) Why does the speaker call the listener?
    (A) To ask him to return some merchandise.
    (B) To invite him to a writing seminar.
    (C) To offer him a membership card.
    (D) To notify him that a book is available.

72. (   ) What can the listener request?
    (A) A private tour.
    (B) Additional time.
    (C) A certificate of completion.
    (D) E-mail notifications.

73. (   ) What does the speaker remind the listener about?
    (A) A charity event.
    (B) Parking restrictions.
    (C) Reduced operating hours.
    (D) An application requirement.

Questions 74 through 76 *refer to the following telephone message.*

Hello, this is Tiffany at Sun Valley Custom Cycle Center. I just heard back from our factory manager about the bicycle you ordered from us last week. It seems that our supplier recently stopped making the seat you'd selected. I looked through our catalog, and I did find some similar seats you might like. They are slightly different designs and materials, though. How about if I e-mail you our supplier catalog and you can take a look and let me know what you think? I'm sorry for the inconvenience.

74. (   ) Where does the speaker most likely work?
    (A) At a furniture store.
    (B) At a real estate company.
    (C) At a construction company.
    (D) At a custom bicycle shop.

75. (   ) What problem does the speaker report?
    (A) An account was mistakenly closed.
    (B) A factory has stopped production.
    (C) A shipment is delayed.
    (D) A component is unavailable.

76. (   ) What does the speaker offer to do?
  (A) Refund a purchase.
  (B) Meet with a customer.
  (C) Send some information
  (D) Negotiate with a supplier.

Questions 77 through 79 refer to the following instructions.

Hey guys, as you know, we've experienced an increasing number of requests for separate checks, even though guests may be dining together. So, before we start tonight's dinner shift, I'd like to show you how to use our new computer system to print guest's bills separately. First, log into the point-of-sale terminal as you normally would by swiping your key card. Then, select the split bills button, which now appears at the left of the screen. This feature will allow you to divide the meals from your tables onto separate bills. There shouldn't be any difficulties, but if there are, Walter's here today.

77. (   ) Where most likely are the listeners?
  (A) At a restaurant.
  (B) At a supermarket.
  (C) At a clothing boutique.
  (D) At a train station.

78. (   ) What are the speaker's instructions mainly about?
  (A) Some staffing assignments.
  (B) Some misplaced equipment.
  (C) A revised corporate policy.
  (D) A computer program feature.

79. (   ) What does the speaker imply when he says, "Walter's here today"?
  (A) Business is slower than usual.
  (B) Staff will be observed by a supervisor.
  (C) Walter made a scheduling mistake.
  (D) Walter can assist with a problem.

Questions 80 through 82 refer to the following excerpt from a meeting.

Before we close today's meeting, I'd like to mention the free wireless Internet service that we are now offering aboard all Orion West Airlines flights. Our competitors offer Wi-Fi, but charge passengers to use it. It is our hope that allowing free Internet access

GO ON TO THE NEXT PAGE.

will ultimately translate to more passengers. Now, I'd like you all to take a few minutes to review a report on the projected budget for the upcoming year and provide your views on whether this proposal is feasible.

80. (   ) What is being discussed?
    (A) Internet availability.
    (B) Staff retention.
    (C) Luggage restrictions.
    (D) Food quality.

81. (   ) What is Orion West Airlines hoping to do?
    (A) Add international destinations.
    (B) Upgrade a computer system.
    (C) Join a partnership.
    (D) Increase ticket sales.

82. (   ) What are the listeners asked to review?
    (A) A budget report.
    (B) A contract.
    (C) A marketing video.
    (D) A newspaper article.

Questions 83 through 85 refer to the following news report.

And now in local events, The Capitol Hill Annual Food Festival is next Saturday and Sunday at restaurants and public venues throughout Lincoln Park and Lower Downtown. The festival attracts hundreds of thousands of visitors every year. You won't want to miss anything, so be sure to check the Web site for a full schedule. One of the most anticipated events of the weekend will be at the Beacon Street Café, where celebrity chef, Jamie Tolliver will do a cooking demonstration and serve a special menu from 4 to 8 p.m.. on Saturday. Plan ahead, as this event is expected to be one of the most popular of the weekend and Beacon Street Café does not take reservations.

83. (   ) What information should the listeners look for on a Web site?
    (A) A traffic update.
    (B) A weather forecast.
    (C) Admission fees.
    (D) An event schedule.

84. (　　) Why is the event at Beacon Street Café expected to be popular?
    (A) A famous chef will be preparing meals.
    (B) The tourism board heavily advertised it.
    (C) A musician will give a concert.
    (D) The restaurant has a good reputation.

85. (　　) Why does the speaker say, "Beacon Street Café does not take reservations"?
    (A) To clarify a policy change.
    (B) To suggest arriving early.
    (C) To criticize a business.
    (D) To propose a different location.

Questions 86 through 88 refer to the following telephone message.

Hi, this is Cole Nordstrom, and I'm the manager at Grayson Manufacturing. Last week, I ordered several parts for a broken water pump and paid an additional fee for express service, but have not yet received the parts. Meanwhile, your Web site tracking system shows that the delivery was made to our factory yesterday, but this is clearly a mistake. Please call me as soon as possible with any information you have about my order. My telephone number is 248-0800. We need the conveyor belt to be working properly so that Fuzuki can meet our customer's deadlines.

86. (　　) What is the purpose of the message?
    (A) To submit an additional order.
    (B) To ask for directions to a factory.
    (C) To request an estimate.
    (D) To complain about a delivery.

87. (　　) Why does the speaker mention a Web site?
    (A) It is difficult to navigate.
    (B) It needs a page for feedback.
    (C) It has incorrect information.
    (D) It is currently inaccessible.

88. (　　) What does the speaker request?
    (A) A copy of an invoice.
    (B) A return telephone call.
    (C) Another machine part.
    (D) A replacement manual.

GO ON TO THE NEXT PAGE

Obviously, the firm is very proud of our team for securing the Spearhead Electronics account. This means we'll be developing the advertising campaign for the client's new line of products. Now, before the hard work begins, the senior managers would like to celebrate by taking the team to dinner. I've come up with three possible dates for the event, and I'd like your feedback. I'll follow up with an e-mail later with the details. Please let me know by the end of the day which date you prefer.

89. (   ) What kind of business do the listeners most likely work for?
    (A) An accounting firm.
    (B) A law office.
    (C) An advertising company.
    (D) A travel agency.

90. (   ) What news does the speaker share with the listeners?
    (A) A ground-breaking ceremony will be held.
    (B) A celebration is being planned.
    (C) An important client will be visiting.
    (D) The department is looking to expand.

91. (   ) What does the speaker ask the listeners to submit by the end of the day?
    (A) Color schemes for a waiting room.
    (B) Requests for vacation leave.
    (C) Time preferences for a dinner.
    (D) Items to include on a budget.

Questions 92 through 94 refer to the following broadcast.

This is Chad Lorimer with Action 12 News, and tonight I'm reporting on an improvement to our city's transportation system that should interest many of our listeners. Commuters have long complained about bus schedules being too complicated and often changing. In response, the Municipal Transportation Department has created a smartphone app you can download to track all public buses. The app will tell you exactly where your bus is located and the approximate time it will reach your stop. No more waiting for a bus, wondering when it will arrive. I'm going to download it today.

92. (   ) What is the main topic of the broadcast?
    (A) A local election.
    (B) A city government building.
    (C) Online advertising.
    (D) Public transportation.

93. (   ) What will the listeners now be able to do?
    (A) Pay a reduced fee.
    (B) Review a document.
    (C) Track some vehicles.
    (D) File a complaint electronically.

94. (   ) Why does the speaker say, "I'm going to download it today"?
    (A) To recommend a service.
    (B) To emphasize a deadline.
    (C) To take responsibility for a task.
    (D) To explain a process.

Questions 95 through 97 *refer to the following announcement and sign.*

Welcome to the 8th Annual Barnum Trails Hike-A-Thon. I'd like to thank KBA Sporting Goods for providing these sun visors which will come in handy at some point in the day. Before starting your hikes, I have a couple of important announcements. As you know, we usually have four hiking trail routes of different lengths. This year, unfortunately, we only have three. The 10-kilometer route is not available today because of emergency bridge work. We apologize for the inconvenience. And lastly, for everyone's safety, let me remind you to always stay on the trails which are marked with bright orange signs along the route.

95. (   ) What is KBA Sporting Goods providing?
    (A) Prizes.
    (B) Refreshments.
    (C) Sports equipment.
    (D) Entertainment.

96. (   ) Look at the graphic. Which route is closed?
    (A) Barnum Edge.
    (B) Barnum Delta.
    (C) Barnum Trek.
    (D) Barnum Ultra.

Barnum Trails Hike-A-Thon	
Barnum Edge	5 kilometers
Barnum Delta	7.5 kilometers
Barnum Trek	10 kilometers
Barnum Ultra	15 kilometers

GO ON TO THE NEXT PAGE.

97. (   ) What are the participants reminded to do?
     (A) Follow designated trail paths.
     (B) Make a donation to an organization.
     (C) Register for an upcoming event.
     (D) Follow the directions of the officials.

Questions 98 through 100 _refer to the following excerpt from a meeting and pie chart._

I appreciate your attendance at today's staff meeting. As you've read in the latest company-wide memo, we have exceeded our forecasted number of sales of our new solar water heater. This high demand is very positive, but it's pushing our production capabilities to their extreme limits. Our factory simply can't meet the new level of demand. To address our shortcomings, we have made an offer to buy one of the smaller, local manufacturers. This company currently holds 40 percent of the northeast region market share. I'm confident that we'll dominate the market in the coming years.

98. (   ) According to the speaker, what was mentioned in the company newsletter?
     (A) Product sales are higher than expected.
     (B) Some executives have retired.
     (C) The company will open offices abroad.
     (D) The company was bought by a larger firm.

99. (   ) What problem does the speaker mention?
     (A) Competition has become more intense.
     (B) Customers are dissatisfied.
     (C) Energy costs have increased.
     (D) The production capacity is limited.

100. (   ) Look at the graphic. Which company may be acquired?
     (A) Reward Auto.
     (B) Innoba.
     (C) Coleman Motors.
     (D) Stepco Industries.

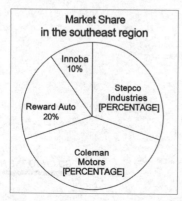

Market Share in the southeast region

Innoba 10%

Stepco Industries [PERCENTAGE]

Reward Auto 20%

Coleman Motors [PERCENTAGE]

NO TEST MATERIAL ON THIS PAGE

GO ON TO THE NEXT PAGE.

New TOEIC Speaking Test

Question 1: Read a Text Aloud

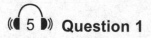 **Question 1**

Directions: In this part of the test, you will read aloud the text on the screen. You will have 45 seconds to prepare. Then you will have 45 seconds to read the text aloud.

Looking for a Chinese restaurant that specializes in traditional Szechuan foods? Then come visit us at Chengdu Garden opening soon on West Park Boulevard. Our menu features the famous spicy Szechuan cuisine. All of our unique dishes are prepared from recipes passed down for generations. The restaurant's opening celebration will take place on October 10 from 5:00 p.m. to 10:00 p.m. There'll be food samples and live music. The first 50 guests will be given a free reusable set of chopsticks with our Chengdu Garden logo. For more information visit our Web site at www.chengdugarden.com.

PREPARATION TIME
00 : 00 : 45

RESPONSE TIME
00 : 00 : 45

Question 2: Read a Text Aloud

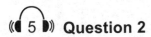 **Question 2**

Directions: In this part of the test, you will read aloud the text on the screen. You will have 45 seconds to prepare. Then you will have 45 seconds to read the text aloud.

This morning, another regional hospital announced that it will be closing its mobile health clinic indefinitely. The mobile clinic was designed to improve access to quality health care for people living in the rural areas outside of the city. According to a spokesperson, the hospital ran a mobile health clinic for ten years until forced to shut it down because of budget cutbacks. As budgets for health care are being slashed across the state, authorities are concerned about rural health care, as fewer people will have access to quality services.

PREPARATION TIME
00 : 00 : 45

RESPONSE TIME
00 : 00 : 45

GO ON TO THE NEXT PAGE.

Question 3: Describe a Picture

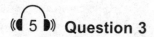 **Question 3**

Directions: In this part of the test, you will describe the picture on your screen in as much detail as you can. You will have 30 seconds to prepare your response. Then you will have 45 seconds to speak about the picture.

PREPARATION TIME
00 : 00 : 30

RESPONSE TIME
00 : 00 : 45

Question 3: Describe a Picture

答題範例

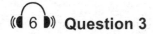

I see a number of people on the street.

This appears to be a film shoot on location.

There is some filming equipment on the sidewalk.

Traffic cones are placed strategically around the scene.

Two men dressed in black appear to be actors.

A car with a siren on the roof is parked haphazardly at the curb.

There are numbered placards on the sidewalk.

Wires and cables run through the street.

There are a number of unidentified objects strewn about.

Several men are standing near or attending to the camera.

Several other people are standing nearby in conversation.

The director appears to be approaching one of the actors.

There is a very large, dark object in the upper-right of the picture.

It's being used to diffuse ambient light.

In the left foreground is a fire escape.

Also in the foreground, a sign offering spa services and massage.

A truck can be seen in the far upper-right corner of the frame.

Someone has spray painted lines around a box in the roadway.

GO ON TO THE NEXT PAGE.

Questions 4-6: Respond to Questions

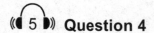 **Question 4**

Directions: In this part of the test, you will answer three questions. For each question, begin responding immediately after you hear a beep. No preparation time is provided. You will have 15 seconds to respond to Questions 4 and 5 and 30 seconds to respond to Question 6.

Imagine that a friend from overseas will be visiting Taiwan. You are having a telephone conversation about his visit.

Question 4

What's the weather like this time of year?

Question 5

What type of clothing is appropriate for sightseeing?

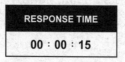

Question 6

If I need to buy clothing during my visit, where should I go, and why?

Questions 4-6: Respond to Questions

答題範例

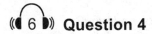 **Question 4**

What's the weather like this time of year?

Answer

> It's summertime.
>
> So, it's going to be very hot.
>
> Also, be prepared for rain.

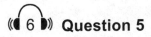 **Question 5**

What type of clothing is appropriate for sightseeing?

Answer

> Light and casual clothing is best.
>
> Most people dress for comfort.
>
> A good pair of walking sandals would be helpful.

GO ON TO THE NEXT PAGE.

Questions 4-6: Respond to Questions

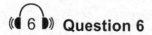 **Question 6**

If I need to buy clothing during my visit, where should I go, and why?

Answer

There are many places to buy cheap clothing here.

The night market is a convenient place to shop for clothing.

You could also go to one of the many malls in the city.

If you have time, there's a special garment district near the

train station.

It's a whole city block of nothing but clothing.

It's almost overwhelming.

A lot of people like to shop at Sogo.

It's a department store that sells all the top brands.

You might want to check it out.

Questions 7-9: Respond to Questions Using Information Provided

 **Question 7**

Directions: In this part of the test, you will answer three questions based on the information provided. You will have 30 seconds to read the information before the questions begin. For each question, begin responding immediately after you hear a beep. No additional preparation time is provided. You will have 15 seconds to respond to Questions 7 and 8 and 30 seconds to respond to Question 9.

EASTER SUNDAY BRUNCH

Please join Taiwanease.com, The Canadian Chamber of Commerce and the Swiss Association of Taiwan for our annual Easter brunch at The Tavern. The last few years have been great affairs. The kids always have a wonderful time, and the parents do too!

As in past years, the event starts at 1:00 PM and goes to 4:00 PM. There will be an Easter egg hunt in the nearby park at 2:00——this is something that the kids love.

The prices are: $550 for adults, $300 for kids over 115 cm, and free for those under!

Full brunch buffet with all your favorites, including carved Easter ham with soft drinks and unlimited coffee and tea from 1:00 to 3:00.

For adults, all draught beers are buy one, get one free.

Program:
1:00 PM to 3:00 PM – Buffet is open
2:00 PM – All kids gather and go to the park for the Easter Egg Hunt
3:00 PM – Egg painting for the kids, supervised by adults

The Tavern is located at 415 Xinyi Road, Section 4

Hi, I'm interested in the Easter Brunch. Would you mind if I asked a few questions?

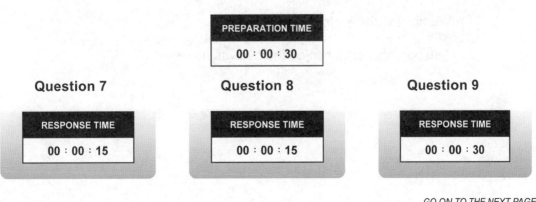

GO ON TO THE NEXT PAGE.

Questions 7-9: Respond to Questions Using Information Provided

答題範例

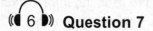 **Question 7**

When does the event take place?

Answer

> The brunch takes place on Easter Sunday.
>
> It starts at 1:00 PM.
>
> It usually ends around 4:00 PM.

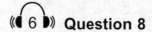 **Question 8**

Who can attend?

Answer

> Anybody!
>
> We have activities for the kids.
>
> And parents usually enjoy themselves as well.

Questions 7-9: Respond to Questions Using Information Provided

 **Question 9**

What is included in the price?

Answer

Well, first of all, there's the food.

It's all you can eat.

The buffet includes Easter ham with soft drinks and

   unlimited coffee and tea.

There will be an Easter egg hunt in the nearby park at

   2:00.

This is something that the kids love.

Adult supervision will be provided.

Finally, there is a drink special.

All draught beers are buy one get, one free.

Hope to see you there!

GO ON TO THE NEXT PAGE.

Question 10: Propose a Solution

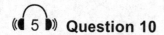 **Question 10**

Directions: In this part of the test, you will be presented with a problem and asked to propose a solution. You will have 30 seconds to prepare. Then you will have 60 seconds to speak. In your response, be sure to show that you recognize the problem, and propose a way of dealing with the problem.

In your response, be sure to

• show that you recognize the caller's problem, and

• propose a way of dealing with the problem.

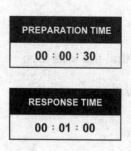

PREPARATION TIME
00 : 00 : 30

RESPONSE TIME
00 : 01 : 00

Question 10: Propose a Solution

答題範例

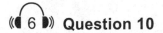 **Question 10**

Voice Message

> Hi Kristen, this is Benjamin. I need to stay in Seattle a couple extra days to finalize this deal. Could you please cancel my flight tonight and book me on a Friday night flight from Seattle to Oklahoma City? Then, I'll need a Sunday evening flight from Oklahoma City home to Chicago. Not too late please. I'll have my wife meet me at the airport, so I won't need a ride. Also, I have a meeting scheduled Monday with Mr. Morgan from Glenn & Glenn. Please phone him and reschedule until Tuesday——no, better make that Wednesday, in case I get delayed in Oklahoma City. For now, don't forward any messages to me unless they're urgent. I'll be in negotiations all day tomorrow and Friday. If you need to reach me, call my cell phone and leave a message. Thanks Kristen. I'll see you Monday morning.

GO ON TO THE NEXT PAGE.

Question 10: Propose a Solution

答題範例

Hi Benjamin, I got your message.

Sorry to hear that you're stuck in Seattle.

I've got things under control in the office.

I got in touch with the airline this morning.

I've got you booked on the 9:30 p.m. flight out of Seattle.

You'll be in Oklahoma City before midnight.

The Sunday evening flight is a bit tricky.

The only evening flight from Oklahoma City leaves at 5:30 p.m.

Is that late enough for you?

I went ahead and canceled your limo on Friday.

They told me there is a 50% late cancellation fee.

Did you know about that?

Meanwhile, I got in touch with Mr. Morgan.

He can't do Wednesday.

So, I scheduled a meeting for Thursday afternoon.

There really hasn't been anything urgent lately.

If there is, I'll let you know.

Call me when you have a minute.

Question 11: Express an Opinion

 **Question 11**

Directions: In this part of the test, you will give your opinion about a specific topic. Be sure to say as much as you can in the time allowed. You will have 15 seconds to prepare. Then you will have 60 seconds to speak.

Some countries are lifting the ban on same-sex marriage. Do you support the idea or oppose it? Give reasons to support your answer.

PREPARATION TIME
00 : 00 : 15

RESPONSE TIME
00 : 01 : 00

GO ON TO THE NEXT PAGE.

Question 11: Express an Opinion

答題範例

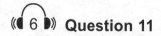 **Question 11**

I fully support the idea.

It is no one else's business if two men or two women want to get married.

Two people who love each other should be allowed to publicly celebrate their commitment.

Same sex couples deserve to receive the same benefits of marriage as opposite sex couples.

Some people say that allowing them to marry threatens the value of "traditional marriage."

However, I believe there is no such thing as traditional marriage.

There are many examples of family arrangements based on polygamy and communal child-rearing.

This is still practiced in many parts of current society.

In that sense, monogamy can be considered "unnatural" in evolutionary terms.

Gay marriage is protected by the Constitution.

The freedom of personal choice is protected by the Due Process Clause.

Therefore, banning gay marriage is unconstitutional.

Denying same-sex couples the right to marry stigmatizes gay and lesbian families.

It implies that it is acceptable to discriminate against them.

It assigns them to second-class status.

Finally, gay marriages can bring financial gain to state and local governments.

Revenue from gay marriage comes from marriage licenses and higher income taxes.

What's more, gay marriage will make it easier for same-sex couples to adopt children.

NO TEST MATERIAL ON THIS PAGE

GO ON TO THE NEXT PAGE.

New TOEIC Writing Test

Questions 1-5: Write a Sentence Based on a Picture

Question 1

Directions: Write ONE sentence based on the picture using the TWO words or phrases under it. You may change the forms of the words and you may use them in any order.

rider / helmet

Questions 1-5: Write a Sentence Based on a Picture

Question 2

Directions: Write ONE sentence based on the picture using the TWO words or phrases under it. You may change the forms of the words and you may use them in any order.

camp / scout

GO ON TO THE NEXT PAGE.

Questions 1-5: Write a Sentence Based on a Picture

Question 3

Directions: Write ONE sentence based on the picture using the TWO words or phrases under it. You may change the forms of the words and you may use them in any order.

dog / stroller

Questions 1-5: Write a Sentence Based on a Picture

Question 4

Directions: Write ONE sentence based on the picture using the TWO words or phrases under it. You may change the forms of the words and you may use them in any order.

passenger / pregnant

GO ON TO THE NEXT PAGE.

Questions 1-5: Write a Sentence Based on a Picture

Question 5

Directions: Write ONE sentence based on the picture using the TWO words or phrases under it. You may change the forms of the words and you may use them in any order.

stairs / students

Questions 6-7: Respond to a written request

Question 6

Directions: Read the e-mail below.

From: Justine Frankl, Director of Personnel
To: David Reedus, CEO
Re: Budget meeting
Sent: April 26

David,

Looking over the budget, I have some concerns. First, while the overall spending for the past three-month period was within our budget, an alarming decrease in the amount spent on recruitment is cause for concern. With peak production starting in June, we need to be fully staffed. Therefore, I would like to schedule a meeting to discuss our workforce outlook for the rest of the year.

The proposed meeting would take place tomorrow at 9:30 a.m. in Conference Room B. Please let me know if you have a scheduling conflict.

Thanks,
Justine

Directions: Write back to Ms. Frankl as Mr. Reedus. Give ONE reason why you cannot attend the meeting, and address her concerns about the budget.

GO ON TO THE NEXT PAGE.

Questions 6-7: Respond to a written request

答題範例

Question 6

Justine,

Unfortunately, I will not be able to attend a meeting tomorrow as I will be attending a sales conference in Chicago through Friday, and will not be back at headquarters until next Monday.

However, I would like to clarify the recruitment situation and explain the dramatic expense decrease. As of the end of February, we had received approximately 300% of our estimated applications for open positions. In other words, we didn't need to recruit any more potential employees. Thus, our expenses were significantly lower. I hope this clears things up.

Sincerely,
David

Questions 6-7: Respond to a written request

Question 7

Directions: Read the e-mail below.

From: Thad Sayer
To: Greg Espinoza
Date: Thursday, July 23
Subject: Phone issues

Greg,

I'm writing to discuss an issue related to my recent move to room 7054. I've taken over Daisy Cooper's old office and phone number, as she has taken an extended leave from work. Apparently, customers were not informed about this, and consequently, I have received, on average, over thirty calls a day from her customer accounts. It appears as though the employee directory has not yet been changed to let them know that: (A) She is not here; and (B) Stan Feldspar is handling her accounts in the meantime. To have to take so many calls that are not intended for me is so time-consuming and distracting. Would it be possible to change the extension number or connect my old extension number 5-7025, to room 7054? I would greatly appreciate your help.

Thank you very much.

Thad Sayer

Directions: Reply as Greg Espinoza and acknowledge but decline Thad Sayer's request. Give ONE reason and ONE possible solution.

GO ON TO THE NEXT PAGE.

答題範例

Question 7

Thad,

I understand your issue and I appreciate you bringing it to my attention.

I'm sure the distractions and interruptions must be frustrating, not to

mention, counter-productive. Unfortunately, I am not able to

accommodate you at this time, as our phone system is due to be

completely overhauled next month, which means, a week from

tomorrow. Therefore, I'm no longer authorized to make changes to

the existing system. The good news is you will be assigned a new,

permanent extension that will follow you wherever you work in the

company. This should make your life a lot easier. In the meantime,

I've updated the company directory, and I've asked Stan Feldspar to

contact all of Daisy's clients and let them know about the change.

Thanks for your patience,

Greg

Questions 8: Write an opinion essay

Question 8

Directions: Read the question below. You have 30 minutes to plan, write, and revise your essay. Typically, an effective response will contain a minimum of 300 words.

Choose one of the following transportation vehicles and explain why you think it has changed people's lives.

- Automobiles
- Bicycles
- Airplanes

GO ON TO THE NEXT PAGE.

Questions 8: Write an opinion essay

答題範例

Question 8

There have been many vehicles since the invention of the wheel that changed the world in many ways, but airplanes have made the greatest impact on the lives of all human beings, be it directly or indirectly. The effect can be felt in almost all types of industry, including travel and tourism, satellite and communication, and business and commerce. Airplanes are now the preferred solution for long-distance travel and thousands of flights are operated in airports around the world every day.

In addition, airplanes changed warfare completely and absolutely, which changed the course of history, many times over. A lot of strategic bombing has been replaced nowadays with cruise missile technology, but tactical bombing still seems to be the norm. There are also drones (remotely piloted unmanned aerial vehicles) which have brought about their own well-known changes to warfare. The impact of war cannot be overstated.

Commercially, jet aircraft revolutionized travel. It killed the ocean liners (ships designed to expeditiously move passengers from a port of origin to a different destination——as opposed to cruise ships, which typically operate to move leisure travelers through a loop back to the point of origin). It makes a trip to the other side of the world (and back) a realistic vacation within the reach of many ordinary people, instead of something reserved for the ultrawealthy with yachts and no jobs. It makes the travel part of emigration across oceans a short flight, instead of a month's long voyage on a ship. It has opened up worldwide markets for perishable goods (the flowers in my supermarket here in the U.S. may have been in Amsterdam the day before, and in the Congo the day before that——try that with the fastest ocean liner).

Light (general aviation) aircraft give so much benefit to their local communities. They include air ambulance helicopters and corporate aircraft that move executives swiftly and efficiently as they manage regional business concerns. In the oil industry, light aircraft efficiently patrol pipelines to watch for leaks, monitor construction activity that could compromise underground pipelines, and bring in parts for critical repairs. They can also provide aerial surveillance of crops and ranch herds in agribusiness. Air travel is at the core of all these benefits.

Another aspect affected by airplanes is pollution, particularly air pollution. Airplanes emit toxic gases while flying and especially during landing and takeoff. These gases demolish the ozone layer, leading to global warming. However, ground access vehicles such as passenger cars and buses just entering and leaving the airport often exceed airplanes as the dominant sources of air pollution at airports.

It is clear that airplanes have changed the world, but it has come at a certain cost.